NEVER INCONSTANT

A SEQUEL TO JANE AUSTEN'S PERSUASION

LYNDSAY CONSTABLE

Quills & Quartos
PUBLISHING

Edited by Katie Jackson and Regina McCaughey-Silvia

On the cover *The Love Letter*, 1834. Artist: Thomas Sully

ISBN 978-1-956613-36-0 (ebook) and 978-1-956613-37-7 (paperback)

To Ryland, whose curious mind and bold spirit always inspire me

CHAPTER ONE

Somersetshire, November 1823

Rummaging through an attic, again—it always seemed to be my lot in life to find, sort, and separate. Not that I minded. I had a nature that enabled me to separate the wheat from the chaff with ease. Life was so much more pleasant when things lived in the places that were designed for them.

Cobwebs snuck under the brim of my cap and tickled my nose. I sneezed violently, several times.

"You need help up there, Mrs Wentworth?" Maude queried from the bottom of the stairs. "Because I can help, if you like, if you really, really want me to."

"No, thank you." Maude was deathly afraid of spiders and their whispery housing. The thought of her up there constantly yipping at every dust ball gave me the start of an aching head.

"I am perfectly capable of finding the wooden play swords on my own. Perhaps you could ensure that the Vile

Rooster has not discovered a new hole in the garden fence? Captain Wentworth puts more confidence in his woodworking abilities than I do."

I moved to the small attic window and peered out. My husband was in the garden chasing a squealing little Freddie around the mulberry tree with arms extended forward, grasping with each step. Both were bundled up against the clear cold of the winter's day.

With a smile, I turned back to the attic. Where could those swords have got to? In our recent and hopefully final move, there had been some confusion with the playthings; the winter had been fierce and a storm had been bearing down. Preparations were not done shipshape, Bristol fashion as they usually were.

Frederick's old navy trunk? I seemed to recall little Freddie putting a few odds and ends in there while he pretended to be preparing for a mighty voyage. He had been muttering to himself about Bonaparte escaping from Elba again and needing to assemble the fleet. So much like his father.

When I opened the lid of the trunk, smells of the sea flooded my senses. A few toys were laid on top, and a few more were poking out from under the clothing and books. I sighed and began to unpack. At the very bottom was Frederick's old captain's jacket. I touched the buttons along the front, remembering a day in 1814—the confusion of his declaration of love and a second proposal of marriage in a warmly written letter, my breathless search for him in the streets of Bath, and our very improper, public embrace.

Those buttons pressing against my chest. His rough cheek on my soft cheek as he whispered in my ear. The memories warmed me against the chill of the attic.

I pulled at the jacket, but it stubbornly refused to leave the chest. Seeing that one of those buttons had wedged itself in a small hole, I gave another yank and the jacket tore loose. The button, clearly ashamed of its recent disobedience, flew through the air and rolled under a shelf of books. I scrambled on the floor, risking the revenge of grumpy spiders, and retrieved the button.

The jacket and button were set aside for later repair. When I returned to the trunk, my eye was arrested by the sight of a plank ajar inside. A false bottom?

I reached down and lifted gently. It wobbled up easily, not very securely in place. Another fine Frederick Wentworth woodworking masterpiece, I thought, smiling. A packet of folded letters, many times secured with red ribbon, lay under the plank. Curious, I pulled it out and untied it to find them all addressed to me, in Frederick's familiar hand.

Miss Anne Elliot
Kellynch Hall
Somersetshire

I should have replaced them. It was improper of me to even pick them up. But they were intended for me. As if in a trance, I opened the top one. It was dated almost eighteen years before, 1806, from that terrible time just after I had broken off my first engagement to Frederick Wentworth. I read.

Miss Anne Elliot,

I expect no returning correspondence from you, madam. I will waste no sleep, lose no appetite, tear out not a lock of my hair over you. Please do not presume that I will be in any way a lesser version of myself due to the cruelty of your heart. You have made your sentiments perfectly clear, and I am pleased to say that my first command on the sloop HMS *Asp* is the ideal tonic for any lingering sentiments I may have in regards to you, Anne Elliot.

I wish I could gloss your behaviour to a fine sheen and forgive you of everything. But for forgiveness, you must look to God and never to me. Those sobs, false I am sure, you played out for me upon breaking off our engagement were worthy of the most exalted theatre boards of Europe. The stage would have been the ideal setting for you. Plays full of artifice. Falsity of face, feelings, and words. Lighting, costumes, rehearsals. These would be your ideal domain.

I wish you the best. Although my heart is not in the words, I write them because I ought.

Captain Frederick Wentworth
HMS Asp

Tears fell. I did nothing to stop them. A sob burst from my chest. I clenched my hand over my mouth and glanced at the stairs to make certain I was still alone. It had been years since I had allowed myself to think of the sorrow Frederick suffered when I ended our engagement. How could I have sacrificed those years with him to please a family that was indifferent to my very existence? Foolish, foolish. At least Lady Russell had advised me to break off our engagement with the best intentions and from a place of genuine solicitude. My family had thought only of their standing in society. If I had only…

No. That was too dark a path to trod. I picked up the next letter. If Frederick had been able to survive those years, the least I could do was look through a small window at all he had endured.

Miss Anne Elliot,

An unlucky fellow plummeted to his death and landed very nearly on my head. It is a common enough accident on a ship. Death is bound to happen through accident, disease, or battle sooner or later. But it was the first death of one of my men as a captain. I was taking my usual turn on the deck in the morning. The sailor was a new recruit and well past the correct age of someone who ought to be going to sea for the first time. We are so desperate for men, especially since the barbaric practice of the press-gangs is now officially abolished, although I have heard some tales that captains still employ it. He had been learning to navigate the rigging and shrouds overhead. He slipped and crushed himself on the deck, a hair's breadth from my feet. I had not jumped back at all. The crew rushed up, tended to him as best they could, but it was too late.

The men stared at me in awe. How could I have been so unflappable? After seeing he was clearly beyond Earthly help, my first thought was how fortunate he was. He is beyond the pain of this world. I looked through the crew manifest to find some name of family that I could notify and send on his pay to, but there was none. No one was waiting for him at home. Was he running from a broken heart? From penury? From crime? I asked the midshipmen to make quiet enquiries among the crew, but few knew anything of him. We all assume the poor fellow must have been Purser Rigged and Parish Damned. I gave him the proper service for a burial at sea and split his pay among the seamen, for which they were grateful. The man will no longer suffer.

My thoughts have turned to this several times in the past few days. No one would suspect, if I tumbled overboard on a rough night or if I fell during an inspection of the rigging. First Lieutenant Conner is competent in his duties and would make a decent captain if I were sewn into my hammock and tossed overboard.

Anne, how can I continue? Two souls such as we, fortunate enough to encounter each other in this wide world, to be forever apart? Why? What am I to do? God have mercy on me.

Captain Frederick Wentworth
HMS Asp

The heavy letter floated down from my weak hands. I covered my face. I would read no more. They were addressed to me, written to me, but perhaps never intended for my eyes. If I proceeded without my husband's permission, I ran the risk of steering my happy marriage into uncertain waters.

CHAPTER TWO

I picked up the two letters I had read and carefully refolded them. The red ribbon slid along my fingers as I retied the packet. With the secured bundle in my hand, I placed Frederick's jacket on top of it. That one, terrible button went in my pocket. I left the attic.

Downstairs, Freddie and his father were in the parlour, each involved in their own important task. My husband read from a book while my son was busy building a fortification of wooden blocks around his paper ships on the floor.

"Mama, I have to secure the harbour, see? Else the French will over, um, overtrod us."

"I think you meant to say *overrun* us."

"Yes, Mama! That too. Both are a bad business. Over-runned and overtrodded. A bad business unless I fortify the harbour wall. Right, Papa?"

Frederick had looked up from his book to supervise the operation. "Right you are, son. Too many times I saw captains neglect simple things they could have done on land to turn the battle in their favour. Good thinking."

Frederick looked up to me with a smile that soon faded. He always knew when I had been upset.

"Son, can you go on an important mission for me?"

"Absolutely!"

"Excellent. Never miss an opportunity to volunteer for a mission, it shows initiative. Now, I heard…" He paused, peering around as if trying to discover a spy. "Betsy was planning on making that raisin pudding of hers."

Freddie popped up clapping.

"I need you to go to the kitchen and see if the rumours have any truth to them. And whether she is putting a bit of pumpkin in it. And, this is the most important part, you must taste it for me and report back."

The little boy solemnly saluted and tore out of the parlour.

Frederick turned to me, his eyes falling on his captain's jacket. "Is something bothering you, my love?"

I lifted his jacket off my hand, exposing the bundle of letters underneath.

Silence hung in the room. His weatherworn, handsome face paled. He leant back in the chair, rubbing his forehead with his hand and shading his eyes from me.

"I read—" I confessed. "I read only the top two. The oldest. I am sorry. I know I ought not to have. But they were addressed to me, and I was curious, and…"

Words failed me.

Frederick finally stood and walked to me. He took the stack of letters from my hand and placed them on the table, then wrapped his arms around me. His lips pressed to mine, starting softly and ending firmly. My heart raced just as it had that fateful day in Bath.

He stepped back and turned to leave the room.

"They are from my first year at sea as a captain. If you wish to continue reading, you have…you have my blessing," he said, pausing with his back to me. "It's solely your choice to make. They are yours, as I wrote and addressed them to you. Their seals have remained unbroken all these years. I apologise for the lateness of their delivery."

Without turning, he left. I looked down at the offensive pile of papers. The fire would do quick work of it. It would make them disappear forever, never to darken our door again. I placed my small hand on top of them, glancing at the cheery blaze in the hearth, unaware of its own power to destroy. My gaze fell back to the letters. How many cannon-balls had they survived? How many hurricanes? Having lived aboard ships with Frederick over the years, I knew how valuable even the smallest bit of space was; only the absolute necessities and his most precious possessions would still be in that locker. No, I could not destroy them.

I picked up the packet and went to the library. It was a small room on a quiet side of the house, farthest away from the kitchen, vegetable garden, and activity of Freddie. I settled into a chair closest to the windows that overlooked a modest rose garden and a pool. Gently removing the ribbon and setting it aside, I took the third letter out and broke its seal.

Miss Anne Elliot,

I was tapping my hard biscuit on my plate at dinner today. I had forgotten I was not totally alone in my cabin. I laughed aloud, thinking of you. Owen, my man, asked if I was all right. I said yes and dismissed him.

Would you still laugh at seeing me bang the plate with a biscuit? That was our very first conversation, if that memory still has any value to you. We both happened to be dining at the home of a parishioner of my brother.

We had never spoken beyond formal addresses. Out of the habit of years at sea, I was tapping my roll on the side of my plate without realising. I stopped and looked around, hoping none had noticed. That is when I first really noticed your eyes. You were staring at me, politely inquisitive as to what I was doing, but not willing to mention it in front of the rest of the company. I simply smiled. You smiled back. Those glittering eyes, that gentle curve of your mouth. That is the moment I thought to myself, 'Here is a woman that I would like to know much better.'

Later in the parlour, we were all having coffee after the meal. Both of us, feeling a special sympathy, I like to think, sought each other out in a quiet corner.

'Was that roll giving you offence in some way that it deserved such punishment, Captain Wentworth?'

I laughed aloud, which made the sparkle in your eyes dance even more.

'Or were you employing the roll as a musical instrument? Are you an admirer of music?'

Your questions were so humorous and intelligent, yet respectful. I was captivated.

When my laughter settled, I told you the roll had committed no offence, I was indeed very fond of music and was probably too fond of the sound of my own voice, although perhaps no one else shared my liking for it.

'Then, if you do not mind my asking, why were you tapping the plate with your roll at the meal?'

'You will not like the answer,' I told you. 'It may be offensive to the ears of a lady.'

You seemed even more intrigued and pressed me further, though with perfect manners.

'I promise, I will not blame you for giving offence. My curiosity will not allow me to slumber this evening if you do not explain this to me. Have compassion for my health, Captain Wentworth.'

I proceeded to tell you that after months at sea, the barrels of biscuits developed an infestation of bargemen, a nice word for weevils and other insects. I tapped the roll out of habit, as we do on our ship to eject the bargemen from our biscuit. Although some of the men develop a taste for them over time and will consume them with the biscuit after spreading them thin with a knife. I have never developed a taste for them and prefer my biscuits to be bargemen-free. And although I had one doctor tell me he suspected the bargemen of helping to maintain good health, I try to rid my meal of as many of them as I possibly can.

I remember waiting for you to swoon or curl a lip in disdain or run back to the company of the other women. But you stood there, fascinated. I stood fascinated as well, though for different reasons, I suspect.

'I see there is more to life in the Royal Navy than I realised,' you responded. 'Please, tell me more of things I am not likely to read in books or newspapers.'

That evening was the happiest of my life. From that moment, your handsome face, eyes blazing with an eager mind, I was gone.

Anne, what could I have done differently? If I could only be completely certain as to why you broke off our engagement. I recall you telling me some nonsense about it being best for my career, that having a wife such as yourself would be a hindrance to furthering my advancement. If I could only see in your heart as clearly as I see your eyes in memories that torment me. My wounded pride prevented me from pursuing you that night you broke our engagement and taking you in my arms, demanding the further explanation that was owed to me. I suspect I am not grand enough for either Lady Russell or your father and sister. Do you feel the same? All I lack is fortune?

I thought you cared little for impressive fortunes as long as there was worthy conversation to be had. I will be rich soon enough. I am a damned good captain with good luck sitting on my shoulder. I feel it in my bones. The men feel it as well. We look eagerly to the horizons for a prize ship to line our pockets with. I am told by my man Owen that I even have a nickname already. Every captain receives one eventually. They refer to me as 'Steely Went' behind my back. I was rather hoping for 'Went n Steel' but did not want to be presumptuous in pushing my own nickname. You will laugh at that bit, when you read it. I can hear it in my mind, like a favourite piece of music.

I wish you well, Anne Elliot.

Captain Frederick Wentworth
  HMS Asp

He was right, I did laugh aloud. 'Went n Steel', indeed. When the laughter subsided, I endeavoured to recall our last meeting before he was assigned the *Asp*. The meeting where I broke off our engagement. It was a painful blur of pale faces, tears, and me wiping my nose with the sleeve of my gown like a child lost in the woods. I placed my hand to my side, remembering the painful stitch there as I ran away. How much had I explained to Frederick? My usually sharp memory recoiled from that day, burnt by the heat of those emotions. I could not recall much of the conversation or the following days that I lay in bed, supposedly indisposed by a headache. I had come dangerously close to surrendering to despair and fading away altogether.

My hand reached for the fourth letter unconsciously. It was unfolded and before my eyes before I had even realised what was happening.

Miss Anne Elliot,

No one advises you that a captain's greatest enemy can be loneliness. I have seen loneliness that led to madness, in some unfortunate cases. I have spent so many years working twice as hard as those around me for recognition and advancement. No one was home forwarding my career using their wealth and connexions. It is difficult to have worked so ceaselessly, to have finally attained the rank of captain and my own modest ship to command, and then realise how lonely it really is.

If I were in the militia on land, I would frequently see other officers of my own rank. I would have had the fellowship of my equals. But here, it could be months, sometimes years before I can have a proper sit-down with a fellow captain. Were I a man of wealth —but this is a dangerous topic to write to you about, is it not? Were I a man of wealth, things would be different, both on land and on the seas. There may have even been a wife writing long, loving letters for me to anticipate. That is not the case, however.

But more to the point, were I a wealthy captain while at sea, I could frequently give lavish dinners for my officers, and we would have the opportunity to eat, drink, and make merry. But, as are all captains, I am required to buy most of my own food for this voyage. My options were limited, due to my aforementioned finances. Thank God my dear sister provided me with the gift of coffee, sugar, and my very own chicken, Theresa. Theresa lives in one of the longboats under a tarpaulin. I save as many of the bargemen I can dislodge from my biscuits so that I may give them to Theresa. She very kindly provides me with eggs in return. Sometimes, Owen hoards up the eggs so that I may have a real meal of several scrambled with a rasher.

I think my uniform has become noticeably looser since we left England. I could abide my poor fare gladly, if only I had the gift of good conversation. Alas, it is not to be. Even on a ship this small, I must keep aloof from everyone, even my officers. There is no more certain way to lose control of your men than to get too friendly. I have seen it before with officers who command the petty officers and seamen. They make awkward overtures of friendship to those of lower rank, and it inevitably ends in a loss of respect from the very ones they wish to befriend. So, my solitary meals must be accompanied by reading one of my few precious books or by the remembrance of lively company of the past.

I see the ghost of you frequently sitting across from me, trying not to laugh at something that I have said that was, of course, enormously clever. I wonder if I will have the courage to post these letters when we reach our assigned port in the West Indies. I would kiss each one before I handed them off for a return voyage to England.

But I begin to realise that these letters may never

see your lovely eyes peering down at them. I write them anyway. I can see the questions forming in your mind. You and your questions! I laugh aloud as I put that to paper. I write to the memories of you, to the memories of us, to the possibilities of what may have been. I write to ease my lonely heart, even though my heart aches terribly with a different sort of pain afterwards. I wish you all the best.

God bless you, Miss Anne Elliot.

Captain Frederick Wentworth
HMS Asp

I sighed as I refolded and placed that fourth letter on the growing pile of those that I had read. The roses past the window were in need of tending. Although it was winter, I could see the neglect they had had at the hands of their former owners and vowed to do my utmost to earn their trust in the coming spring. It would be a sweet spot for reading at the height of summer.

Loneliness. I knew something about that. To be lonely in a crowded room or a crowded ship. To be unable to speak to others due to such a great difference in temperament and intellect as to make a real conversation an impossibility. I was very familiar with what he described. In Frederick's case, rank and discipline necessitated it. In my case, a house ruled by my sister and father made self-imposed isolation the only path to survival. I did have interludes with my friend, Lady Russell, which helped me to keep my reason. Frederick and I both had been through a special kind of isolation that bound our hearts even more powerfully to one another. Of all the vivid hardships that I had imagined for my husband through the years of our separation, loneliness had not even occurred to me. In fact, I had foolishly thought that the camaraderie of naval life would have eased his pain. I had been completely mistaken.

My conscience pricked as another wound of my unintentional infliction sprung up on the scarred heart of my dear Frederick. Had I kept the engagement, had I not been persuaded to break it, he would have at least had the modest comfort of many letters filled with love from his wife during his long years at sea. Most likely, I would have accompanied him on several occasions for voyages across the seas.

My temper, usually so calm, flared briefly at the cruel injustice done by family and friends upon us. I sprang up and opened the door to the rose garden. The chill air of the sunny winter day freshened my face. I stepped out and took several turns in the walled, secluded spot. The roses lacked foliage, but still had their thorns. I gently touched one of the sharp points. Seemingly dead, but still ready to defend itself so that it may spring to life again at just the right time. I smiled with admiration at the plant. The love I had with Frederick had survived a cruel winter and sprang back to life again. So would the roses.

CHAPTER THREE

Miss Anne Elliot,

Well, my heart has been won by another. You have been officially replaced as the foremost queen in my affections. It happened so slowly that it was upon me before I realised what had occurred. If you could only meet her, you would see how irresistible she really is. Some may call her an old maid, but, while the bloom of her glory days is definitely in her wake, she can still beguile. Oh, I should have guarded more closely whom I give my love to. I am apt to call myself inconstant with how quickly a love so deep for you has been conquered and vanquished by another.

Are you the least bit curious? Do I take my teasing too far, as you have, on occasion, reprimanded me for in the past? But how often did my teasing lead to that most precious of all gifts you had in your power to dispense, your laughter? I crave to hear that sound one more time, above all others. My new ladylove has so many admirable qualities, but mirth is not among them. And yet, even without the gift of humour, she stole my heart. Must you know her identity?

Very well, since you demand satisfaction, the lady I now love with all my heart is the dear old HMS *Asp*. She is willing and answers all my commands. Her eighteen guns on but a single deck deliver a punch that will leave much larger ships breathless. I finally got to let her show me her best today and am a richer man for it.

Before sunrise, as the sky was just beginning to lighten, a ship was spotted due west. Whether they saw us and judged us not a threat or a trick of the eyes looking towards the rising sun or a sleeping seaman neglected his lookout duties, I know not to what we owed our scratch of luck. The wind was to our backs, and we gained on them. Even if they knew of our presence, the rising sun at our aft would have made it difficult to judge our approach or see whose flag we flew. You see, even if they could have got a good look at us, the wind was sweeping our flags forwards making it difficult to see the Union Jack.

We were upon that French privateer before she really had time to make any sort of rational change of course. Our guns were out, and we let off a volley almost broadside that de-masted her immediately. A lucky shot, that. The thrill of seeing their mast topple down! The frigate let off a half-hearted volley that caused us minimal damage. They appeared not to be practised at aiming or firing simultaneously.

Again, we sent a perfectly timed volley at them after my men had reloaded at lightning speed. Every gun on the starboard side fired in unison, sending the little *Asp* careening to the port side from the recoil. It was a joyous moment. All those hours of practise at sea, the waste of powder, it paid off. Their captain ran up the white flag, and we boarded with nothing more than a few scraped knees and black eyes.

Once we repaired it, rechristened it, and installed a small crew of men from the *Asp*, we sent her back to England as our very first (but not last) prize ship. It will be a fine, fine payment to us. On board were some very valuable goods, such as wines and bolts of cotton and silk, some of them being highly valued indigo. Even from this small first prize, my fortune will be elevated enough that I will no longer be shamed by my betters due to my lack of funds.

Of the men on the ship that captures a prize ship, the captain receives the largest share. It is a significant increase from my shares as a first lieutenant. I have no hopes of ever meeting the standards of wealth and prestige required by your family and acquaintances, Anne, but my fortunes have risen high enough that the next time I propose marriage to someone above my station, it will not be a source of ridicule and amusement by the intimates of the lady.

But that day of happiness is years in the future. For now, I talk and think of only the *Asp*, she who loves me so dearly as to risk all for my sake. I am a fortunate man.

Captain Frederick Wentworth
HMS Asp

I f anyone had ever told me, 'One day, you will feel jealous of a ship', I would have had to refrain from laughing in their face. To read those words of admiration and affection, words that had I chosen differently for myself would have been written to me, filled me with actual envy. I really did pause and laugh at myself.

How did he do it? Frederick had always possessed the ability to make me laugh, even from the earliest moments of our acquaintance. I remembered that very first dinner party, the sound of my own laughter startling me because my ears were so unused to it. I had actually looked around to see if any had noticed because it was so rare an occurrence. Back then, my pleasantest days were filled with quiet, reflective conversation with Lady Russell. The most unpleasant of my days were filled with forced smiles and nodding at the supercilious observations of my father or the vicious cuts of my sister. Within my limited social activities prior to meeting Frederick Wentworth, I had met those whose wit I had admired. Even those who gave rise to a gentle chuckle from me. But to really, fully laugh?

My smile faded as I tried to recall laughing deeply and fully at any time before meeting Frederick. Perhaps when my beloved mother had still been alive? I suddenly recollected fits of laughter that my father had frowned upon.

"Terrible wrinkles befall those who laugh, Anne" had been Sir Walter's fatherly advice upon observing any mirth from me. "The wrinkles that follow the laughter are the first step down the unhappy road of a dissolute countenance. Many young women, I have observed, have a glowing, unblemished air to their skin and then, tragedy strikes! Laughter, too readily, too frequently. And what do you think the result may be? Thick lines down each side of the nose, crow's feet, even a puckering between the brows! Nay, nay, nay. Not in any daughter of mine, please. It would be a positive abomination! Look to your sister Elizabeth. She never laughs. Her smiles are bestowed but rarely. The reward for such restraint? Observe the smooth perfection of her skin! Not a trace of lines from the abuse of laughter can be observed anywhere upon her countenance. So, heed my wisdom, think long and hard on the severe consequences of laughter, Anne. Let Elizabeth be the example that you endeavour to emulate. She is the model of womanly perfection."

I walked to a mirror and gazed with an honest, critical eye. I possessed all the hallmarks of the wickedness of frequent laughter on my face. How Father must cringe when he sees me! Perhaps that was why he has so earnestly pressed for the use of Gowland's Lotion for my face.

I smiled when my thoughts drifted back to the culprits of those wrinkles: Frederick Wentworth, and now his son was included in that party as well. I relished each fold in my skin and hoped for many more from the same causes.

I sat back down and picked up my next letter.

Miss Anne Elliot,

Today I discovered a sound that I did not even realise that I hungered for even more ardently than your laughter. I heard your name spoken aloud. Halfway round the world, almost to the West Indies, and I heard your name pass the lips of another.

I wonder, did the mighty wind gust it back to you all the way in England? Did you hear it whispered on the breeze? Hearing the words 'Miss Anne Elliot' spoken, it was like God himself had reached a hand down and given me a shake as if I were a child's rag doll. One of the ship's quartermasters, a Mr William Rollins, had the fortune of being mildly acquainted with your family his whole life. Do you recall the name? A small farm family within the range of Kellynch Hall and your gracious charity.

When we found we had both spent time in the same

neighbourhood, I encouraged the nervous young man to speak of your family. His remarks on your father and sisters were polite and exceedingly guarded. But when he spoke of you, Anne, I expect your ears burnt to a crisp, for the praises were numerous and sincere. Apparently, the family credits your intervention with a gift of fresh fruit and medicines for the salvation of his youngest sister, Letty. He was emphatic in his declaration that had you not visited frequently, Letty would have returned to the embrace of the Lord. Your hurried fetching of the doctor saved her from death.

Of all the ships in the fleet he could have been posted to, William Rollins is on mine. I vacillate between gratitude and bitterness, my heart being unable to make one of those its home. I must absolutely refrain from begging this man to say your name over and over again. It would tear me to shreds. After my chat with young Rollins, I deliberately stood with my face full to the gusting wind, my ears roaring with the sounds of the sea, so I could attempt to drown thoughts of you out of my head.

I am one of the strongest officers in His Majesty's Navy—strong of body, mind, and courage. You know me too well to imagine me a braggart; I am simply stating the fact. But I begin to think I may not have the strength to overcome memories of you, Anne. Even my beloved *Asp*, with all her glories, is but a faint candle next to you.

Captain Frederick Wentworth
  HMS Asp

I recalled the Rollinses and their dear little Letty. In some of the darker corners of the cottage, there had been the shuffling sounds of several other children. William Rollins must have been one of them. My heart felt content that I had been of real service to them in a time of need. My father and eldest sister had been generally indifferent to the sufferings of their tenants and the surrounding families, a fault that I have always endeavoured to correct in any small way that was within my power. My kindness had been repaid by the unconscious act of William Rollins speaking my name aloud to the comfort of Frederick's ears and heart as they travelled across a sea.

"Frederick Wentworth, Frederick Wentworth," I whispered quietly to the empty library that had become misted in the shadows of the setting sun. The flavour of those words on my tongue was just as sweet that evening as they had been long ago.

I remembered too clearly, in those horrible years after I had broken off our engagement, how desperately I wanted to speak of him to someone. *Anyone.* Just to say his name or hear it being spoken aloud. But, no. It could not be. Lady Russell went into pontifications of moral fortitude if I ever even hinted about missing Frederick or feeling deep regret at the broken engagement. Father and Elizabeth never even acknowledged that the affair had ever occurred. His name never crossed their lips. I believed, within a few months, the entire incident had vanished from their memories. My younger sister Mary had no knowledge of his existence due to being away at school for the entirety of our brief courtship and even briefer engagement.

What a marvel it was that Frederick and I had been at opposite ends of the earth, yet each of us was desperate to hear the other's name spoken and was craving to speak the other's name.

Dinner that night was a quiet affair.

Frederick seemed not willing to look me in the eye as frequently as usual. There was a hush of unspoken thoughts that made the dining room heavy, and little Freddie was quite worn out from his jaunting about with his father that day.

I spent a good bit of time preparing our son for bed, reading to him, kissing him, tucking him in for the night. His tousled hair smelled of sunshine and secrets.

"Mama?"

"Yes, love?"

"Is Papa planning a big battle with the enemy?"

Laughing, I smoothed his locks from his forehead. "Not to my knowledge. I imagine any enemy would be far too scared of your papa to plot an invasion. Why do you ask?"

"We had a jolly time, but he got quiet sometimes and looked far away, at the clouds."

"Well, that is just how fathers get sometimes, you know. Now to sleep with you, love." I gave him a final kiss on the head before quietly leaving his room.

I entered our bedroom silently. Frederick was already asleep in bed, lying on his side, his broad back turned towards me. I undressed, combed my hair, and slipped delicately under the counterpane.

He did not stir. I slid closer. I curved my body around his, my cheek pressed between his shoulder blades. My hand reached under his night shirt and traced a long, jagged scar that ran down his right lower back. I bit my lip at the physical reminder of a time he had almost left me alone in this world. To chase that thought away, I slid my hand along the smooth parts of the skin of his back, carefully avoiding other smaller scars that were scattered across his body. I did not want to think of what might have been. I did not want him to think of such things, either.

A shuddering breath entered his barrel chest. He rolled over and faced me. He reached his hand up to my face and stroked my cheek.

"Anne..."

"Frederick..."

His lips pressed to mine and we were suffused with a passionate, blind melting into one another. Like two ship-wreck survivors weathering a storm raging around them, our entire world was each other.

CHAPTER FOUR

The next morning, Frederick announced that he and Freddie were bound to go to the Crofts at Kellynch and asked if I would join them. Mrs Sophia Croft had been eagerly awaiting a visit; she could not leave Admiral Croft as he suffered from his gout. Without children of her own, she took the role of aunt very seriously. I expressed some trepidation at the coolness of the weather and the possibility of being snowed in. As usual, they took this clucking of concern as encouragement towards adventure.

"I think it a capital idea that the two of you visit the Crofts. I will decline joining you, for you know how much I dislike the cold ever since those few months aboard a ship in the Baltic Sea. And your trip will also provide me with some silence for my reading. Should the carriage be readied?" I asked.

"For a journey of five miles?" Frederick replied with a laugh. "I think my son and I are capable of a brisk ride for an hour. It is cool, I grant you, but the sun shines bright. What say you, son? Will you be my first lieutenant on this bold voyage?"

Freddie's eyes shined with eagerness as he nodded vigorously. Had his father suggested a quick jaunt to France, riding on horseback over the Channel the entire way, he would have seen no harm in the quest and readily agreed.

"Besides, Anne, that is the very reason we settled here in this snug manor house. We are within close distance to those we love best. Two miles from Uppercross, five miles from Kellynch, and half a day's journey to Lyme. It is high time the Wentworth men gave full sail from this safe harbour and tested the roads. What do you say, Freddie?"

"Yes, sir!"

Frederick gave his son a clap on the back. "There's a good man. Now go ask Betsy to wrap up some bread and cheese for our voyage. Never venture into dangerous waters without provisions, remember that, son."

Freddie tore out of the room on his mission.

"And I had better make sure that he puts his thick jacket on and that winter hat," I said as I made for the door. "Fortunately, we unpacked all the winter things right when we arrived…"

Frederick's strong hand shot out and grabbed my wrist, pulling me into his arms. His lips pressed to mine before I could make protestations in favour of my mission to bundle up our son.

"Maude will see that our son is wrapped up watertight, you know that." He growled at me when I tried to wiggle away. "If we do have to berth at Kellynch for the night, I need a few more kisses to tide me over."

My husband proceeded to store away enough kisses to last all the months of winter before they both bustled out the door in a whirl of scuffling shoes, shouts, and goodbyes.

After settling a few household concerns with Maude and

rearranging the size of the day's meals with Betsy, I settled into the library again to whittle down the stack of unread letters from the Frederick Wentworth of the past.

Miss Anne Elliot,

We have come to port at Charlotte Amalie, the capital of St Thomas. As I am sure the newspapers have proclaimed by now, the Danish fleet just recently left and the British takeover of the three islands was bloodless. I had the vital duty of giving a bag of mail from home to the HMS *Seagull* and meeting with her captain before they made their return voyage to England. The bigger guns of the frigate *Seagull* are wanted to help with the blockades of France. We are to stay here with our small but swift sloop to help hold our claim on the islands and overtake as many privateer and pirate ships as possible as prizes.

These waters teem with privateers always on the prowl to steal valuable cargo being shipped to England from the West Indies and the Americas. It is a lucky first assignment for a low-ranking master and commander such as myself. Swift fortunes are made in these waters by a captain and crew who are bold enough to work for it. Even though the *Asp* was rated only for home service before we left England, it handled the voyage across the Atlantic admirably. The blessing of fine weather has been upon us ever since we left home. Now we begin the business of capturing as many pirates and privateers as we can.

My loneliness from the voyage has subsided somewhat. I had several dinners with Captain Fowler of the *Seagull* before their departure. His man was an excellent cook who had the benefit of quality meat and fresh vegetables to work with. Fowler seemed pleasant enough, but perhaps too fond of drink and noisy exclamations with no real wit, for my taste. We discussed the difficulties of keeping a ship of men safe from the ever-present dangers of disease and boredom, the two most vicious enemies on the open sea. He had heard I was an unmarried man and chose to advise me.

'Be forewarned. The mothers of all the young women of this port will undoubtedly have their weather eye on you, sir. They have had only my officers to titter over, a generally feckless group of young bucks, not worth much notice in my opinion. But you'—here he paused to chuckle and take a long, deep draught of his wine glass—'a dashing, young, single captain. Just fallen into one of the choicest spots a navy ship can be in to snatch up privateers and shore up your wealth. You'll be just as valuable as any prize ship you are likely to bag! I feel you ought to be placed on notice that the ladies of this port will be circling you the second you step foot on land.'

At this point in our dinner, I suspected Captain Fowler had had far more wine than was prudent. Nobody would ever accuse him of strict sobriety or a brilliant mind.

I later came to know from my man Owen that this excess in drink was a daily occurrence. The manservants who work for the captains like to exchange tales among themselves when the opportunity arises. It is a valuable way to glean intelligence before you are compelled to go into battle with other captains, for knowing how they may act during times of crises is valuable information that could save the lives of your men.

Captain Fowler talked long of the various schemes

that an unwed captain must maintain his vigilance against. I laughed it off as best I could, but not being so many sheets to the wind as he, I could not help but brood on the past.

You had not cared a bit about my fortune, had you Anne? Even if I were to have remained a poverty-stricken captain with no luck at catching prize ships, I know in my heart you would have looked at me with the same deep, unwavering affection every morning we would have awoken together.

My mind has been so focused on creating my fortune through shrewdness and advancement, I have never stopped to consider that I would never again know the love of a woman for just myself, without rank and wealth. The thought cast a shadow on what I had been anticipating to be one of the pleasantest dinners I had spent in over a month.

'Have you got a betrothed waiting for you at home?' Fowler continued, along the same line. 'Or is your heart free for the taking?'

I did not know how to answer the latter question, so I only replied to the former.

'I am unattached, Captain Fowler.'

To my infinite regret, I added silently to no one but myself.

The next day, the *Seagull* was preparing to return to England. The purser of the *Asp*, Warrant Officer Smith, came to gather any letters that I wished to send in the bag that was to accompany the *Seagull*. I had spent a fretful night. Despite my stomach finally feeling full from Captain Fowler's extravagant dinner, I was restless with the thought of what should befall the letters that I have written to you, Anne. My heart was heavy with the thoughts, food, and wine of the night before.

I had your letters hidden behind a book on my small desk. They were not included with the stack of correspondence that I had already handed to Smith. I stared hard at the book as Smith hovered, waiting to be dismissed to take the launch over to HMS *Seagull*.

I had spent the entire previous night wrestling with regret. Regret at my foolish pride preventing me from fighting harder for you. Regret that I had not convinced you into an elopement.

Just when I thought I had regret pinned and beaten, it escaped, being sly and wily, and came back to torment me further into the night. When I heard the six bells in the early morning hours, a realisation swam over me like a rogue wave. I had nothing of you in my possession. No letters, for every small note you so timidly wrote to me I had burnt in a fit of fury less than an hour after you had broken our engagement.

My rage back then could not foresee a day when I would desire nothing more than to see your neat, elegant hand across a page. Our acquaintance was so short that we'd had no portrait of you made. Had I been a more pressing, bold suitor, I would have demanded a lock of your hair the moment you accepted my proposal of marriage. I am not sure my insistence would have swayed you into doing such an improper thing, but there is a small chance that I could have laughed you into it. I could almost always laugh you into changing your mind on any subject—except for one instance, the most important instance.

Smith cleared his throat quietly, hoping to cajole me into action, no doubt. I knew the tide was favourable for the *Seagull* to leave within the hour. Yet, I remained immobile. Every fibre of my being wanted to send these letters to you. It would have been so easy to shove them into Smith's waiting hand.

All I have left of you is these letters. I wrote them for you, although you will never see them. It is a sad, thin shadow to be haunted by, but at least it is something. It is everything, Anne.

I waved Smith's dismissal. He knuckled his forehead and left quickly. I pulled the stack of letters from behind the book. The little stack felt heavy and dry in my hand. I raised them to my lips and kissed them. I hope some whisper of my kiss reached you, halfway round the world, dearest Anne.

Yours truly,
Captain Frederick Wentworth
HMS Asp

My own hand reached up to brush my fingertips across my lips, so recently pressed by Frederick's farewell kisses and his urgent passion of the previous night. The pads of my fingers left my lips and rested on the thin pile of read letters on the table beside me. Did some trace of his kiss from so many years ago linger on the paper?

I looked up and was surprised by the lightness that greeted me. A substantial dusting of white covered the world outside. During my reading, clouds had rolled in. My heart leapt to my throat as my mind instantly imagined every manner of danger that riding a horse through snow could produce. But my sensible nature took the reins away from the folly of worry. They had had ample time to arrive at Kellynch before the winds brought these rapidly piling flurries. And had any minor impediment arose, I could not imagine a more capable guardian for our son than my husband. I leant back into the cushions of my chair and silently watched the flakes fall.

I awoke later from my unintended nap when Maude brought in a tray of tea. I hurriedly snatched the precious papers away as she clinked down the tray. Her ruddy, round face turned towards the library windows as she peered at the drifts gathering along the borders of the rose garden.

"Well, ma'am, it's a lucky thing we bundled young Freddie up so well this morning, is it not? I expect he'll have a bright red nose for the rest of the day. The snowfalls are so early this year! It only being November and all."

"Yes, winter seems to be making a rather grand entrance." I felt certain then that my husband and son would not return home till tomorrow.

Maude busied herself building up the fire, then closed the door softly behind her. I stood and pulled the letters out from under my shawl where I had hidden them. I felt so protective of these sheets that had been around the world. They were like loyal friends that had been Frederick's only source of solace during the dark days after the dissolution of our engagement. I reflected back on my one and only source of solace.

I went to the bookcase and pulled out the wedding present my father had given us: *The Baronetage*. A large book with a blood-red cover and gold lettering, it held the history of the British nobility within its pages. Sir Walter, who held it to be the holiest of holies, had been so good as to grace its pages with the handwritten addition of our marriage under the entry of the Elliot family. As meagre a sign of affection as it was, I had found it touching. From Father, it was as close a blessing of approbation for the marriage of Frederick and myself as I was likely ever to receive. I had smiled when my father placed the solemn tome in my hands with reverence, as if he were placing the Holy Grail in my care. Glancing at Frederick, only I had noticed his jaw muscles working furiously to contain his disgust of the book. So much pain had arisen from his family not being mentioned among the pages. And only his wealth and distinction from his naval career had made our marriage finally acceptable in my family's eyes.

I placed the book on the table, and it fell open to the exact page where the Elliot family entry was located. There, a slender stack of papers folded to resemble all manner of ships slid out. My precious letters from Frederick from that sliver of time when we were both so ecstatically happy after he had first proposed marriage in 1806 and before he had asked permission from my father. I remembered it so well; we were so very young and desperately in love. His proposal had been so sudden, so unplanned. We had been huddled together near the coats hanging by the front door after a dinner at his brother's house. Those few seconds we were separate from the rest while he helped me don my cloak, our bodies obscured by the darkness of the hall. Frederick murmured in my ear. I had turned and clasped his hands, saying "Yes!" before he had even properly finished the question. He had crushed me into his arms and pressed a quick, urgent kiss to my cheek. The bustle of the other guests had caused us to separate quickly and turn away to hide the burning of our cheeks.

Father was in London with Elizabeth at the time. Frederick had easily convinced me that it was best to wait for Father's return before he applied for permission to marry me. Did Frederick foresee stormy weather? Looking back, I perceived that he wanted those few happy weeks we kept our engagement secret from the world. He must have been aware of the possibility of a heart-crushing refusal. As improper as it was to keep the secret and accept the letters, under mild protest, I now realised that at least I had had the small blessing of these letters to ease the pain of my heart for the eight years between our first and second engagements. Frederick, lonely on the other side of the world, had had nothing save the letters he wrote to me.

I twirled one of the paper vessels between my fingers. He had found the most cunning methods for slipping them to me. Tucking them in a bonnet. Wrapped in my shawl. Slipped in a glove. It was such fun to discover them. Even more fun to scold Frederick for the impropriety of it. His rakish smile and twinkling eyes had revealed the encouragement he sought in the reprimands to commit the minor offence again and again. I took my paper-boat letters and reunited them with their long-lost brethren on the table, next to the tea tray. Before picking up the next unread letter, I lit a candle to dispel some of the eerie twilight of a snowy evening.

My dear Anne,

I wonder what your thoughts would have been had you seen me this evening, in my dress uniform, dancing with the prettiest girls who inhabit the capital of St Thomas. Once I had forced myself to ignore the stifling heat that lingers in every corner of this island even well after the sun has set, I managed to have quite a pleasant enough evening.

Some of the young women are indeed exceedingly lovely, as Captain Fowler had warned me. But the entire evening went by and I trod on not a single foot. By the end of the evening, it was general knowledge that I was the finest dancer that the British navy had ever produced. You never got to see me in such fine form. Are you shocked? Do you believe I may be untruthful? You insult me, Anne.

It is the sad truth that not one of the young ladies had me so entranced, so bewitched that I stomped on a foot during a dance. As you know well from our first dance together, only the most beautiful eyes and sparkling wit make me a clumsy oaf. How many times did I scuff your slippers? Did your maid ever mend that rent in the hem of your yellow gown that I caused? I loved the colour yellow on you.

Only you, Anne, ever had that effect on me. I can see you so clearly to this day, how ardently you repressed your laugh at my missteps. You were too kind to let one of those smiles reach your lips. The smiles filled your eyes, though.

I wish I could put all these scheming daughters and mothers of St Thomas at ease. If only they knew that a sign of true affection from me results in bruised toes and damaged hems, I am not so sure they would gaze at me with such ardour, especially if I were to wreak such havoc on their wardrobes and slippers.

One persistent, comely young woman, Catherine LaCroix, daughter of the governor, had the look of a cat steadily soft-stepping towards her prey as she gazed at me from across the ballroom. Her eyes hardly left me the entire evening. I must confess, between her stunning face and quick wit, there was a time when I would have probably stumbled when dancing with her. She is an accomplished, lovely young woman who would grace the arm well of any navy officer lucky enough to catch her eye. And it was even whispered to me, no doubt by design in case my mind worked on such issues, that her inheritance is substantial.

Alas, it is all too late for Miss LaCroix. All of those timed tosses of her bouncing yellow curls, the fluttering of her fan just above her low-cut bodice to attract my eye to her ample bosom, the smoky stares out from under long lashes, it was all lost on me, though I did find it amusing—and, if I must be perfectly honest, flattering. But through her graces, I sensed a heart where ambition sat high on the throne as ruler. Had my fortune, prospects, or face been less attractive, her interest would have been a fleeting sneer. A hard heart makes all charms wither, like a winter wind curling under the browning leaves of a rose.

My ship is now well restocked with provisions, and we have not lost a single seaman to desertion. I hope that speaks well to my abilities as a captain to treat those under me with fairness. The men seem to have developed a begrudging affection for 'Steely Went'. I am actually looking forward to returning to sea and pursuing privateers and pirates for the enrichment of His Majesty's Navy and to make the seas a safer place in which to do commerce.

I wish I could see how you are faring, Anne. Has another won your heart already? Are you well? Are you happy? I asked William Rollins about the state of his family's health back in Somersetshire when I saw that he received several letters from home. I was hoping he would let slip any information about you or your family. Alas, he did not.

Seeing all these young ladies displaying their accomplishments and beauty in an effort to turn my head has only given rise to thoughts of you. Perhaps, someday soon, I will enter a ball with no thought of the past and what might have been. For now, the sea is my only solace. The only women who have my daily affection are the *Asp* and Theresa, the chicken.

Yours,

Captain Frederick 'Steely Went' Wentworth

HMS Asp

The red embers in the grate suddenly shifted and collapsed, sending a bouquet of yellow and red sparks flying up the chimney. My candle was almost out. The windows were black from the moonless night. Snow curved round the sills. A chill shuddered up my spine at the thought of those first few months after Frederick returned to sea when our engagement was shattered by the heavy weight of disapproving family and friends.

I had fared little better than Frederick. At least he had the comfort of hard work to help numb himself to the pain of his heart. Activity that could distract from the reminders of what might have been had we been allowed to marry. But, as a lady, I had only time and silence to relive my thoughts of our past acquaintance. I remembered slowly walking through all the locations that witnessed our happy scenes together, my heart bursting with sorrow. Aside from a brief stint to the city of Bath with my father, there had been no relief, change in scenery, or flurry of activity to give my mind pause from the constant swirl of regrets. I was glad, at least, that I had been fortunate enough to possess the fortitude to survive. That was about all I could claim of that time —that I survived.

CHAPTER FIVE

Although night pressed in, I simply had to continue with my reading. I took a candle from the mantel and replaced my sputtering stub with it. What had become of the formidable Catherine LaCroix? In spite of her attempts at Frederick, I wished her well. I would give her the benefit of the doubt, that any woman would have found my Frederick irresistible, the status of his fortune notwithstanding.

The new candle glowed to the fullest brilliance it could muster. I chose the next letter, cocooned my shoulders in my shawl, and opened it. The red seal, warmed and pressed into place to close the papers so many years ago, snapped when I slid my finger under it.

Dear Anne,

Were you here to see the wonders of this part of the world, you would marvel at the many miracles God's hand has wrought upon this earth. You, who have lived a full life through your extensive reading of poetry and prose, would have so much to say if you could but witness the power of Mother Nature here in these islands.

I know my keen mind has a talent for a quick turn of phrase to make those around me laugh, but I do not possess the patience to attain your deeper understanding of the inner lives of those around me and the beauty of the natural world through the writings of others. I like to think that my short time with you did help to cultivate that part of me. When I write to you, I do attempt to turn a phrase in a way that you would appreciate. Sometimes, as I walk the decks, during a spectacular sunset or as our ship slices among a racing pod of dolphins, I cannot help but ask myself, 'What would Anne say, if she were here by my side?'

Just the other day, the *Asp* was witness to a sight few can boast of having seen. I noticed the next day, even the most hardened of seamen were more solemn during Sunday's church service.

When the sun had passed its summit and was declining off to the west, there was a solid bank of clouds off our port bow. It looked like it was moving rapidly towards us, but no squally weather ran before it, so I took only a mild interest and informed the man in the crow's nest to keep his weather eye upon it and that I should be informed of any developments immediately.

I had just gone to my cabin for some lunch when I heard a shout and the pounding of feet on deck. I stayed seated, despite being damned curious. Nothing shows a captain's weakness of mind more than an eagerness displayed before the men. It makes them unsure of your capacity to keep your calm in a combat situation. First Lieutenant Conner came into my cabin, asking permission to speak. He related that 'something' was off the port bow that required my attention. I gave a good show of grumbling about the interruption and followed him slowly.

There, in the distance, far away but not far enough for my ease, were two towers snaking towards us. I wish you had been there, Anne, to see it. My words can hardly do it justice. It makes my heart flutter at the remembrance of such a display. The rotating towers stretched up, from the water to the sky far above. The men began to mumble uneasily. I gave a curt look to Conner. 'Quiet there, below decks!' he bellowed.

My heart raced and seemed to move up to my mouth as I gazed calmly at the twin goliaths.

'Ah,' I said, ''tis nothing more than a few water-spouts. Wind and rain in a tower, running together before that bank of clouds.' As I nonchalantly informed those around me of the nature of the beasts, before our eyes another spout reached up from the sea and reached down from the sky to meet in the middle. An audible gasp emerged.

I gave orders for the boat to take a hard northeast port tack to hopefully outrun the line of windy troops hoping to overtake us. The boatswain whistled out instructions, the sails on the starboard side of the boat unfurled fully, and the *Asp* lurched ahead, gaining speed. I heard her straining under the pressure, her beams groaned in protest, but nothing to alarm. The strengthening wind made the ropes in the rigging sing in a high-pitched wail. I calmly strolled to the aft of the ship to supervise our unwanted visitors. I muttered to Conner to whip the men into shape and get them back to their duties. He should have known to do that on his own, but he, too, was entranced by this glorious show of pure power by Mother Nature.

A few hours later, we eventually outran the persistent pursuers, each spout withering and fading. Within earshot of some of the seamen and midshipmen, I said to Conner, 'Well, then, I'll be off to dinner now, so notify me if anything of true interest occurs. Lovely set of waterspouts, eh?' Once I reached my cabin, I loosened my jacket and sighed. My relief at the *Asp* being spared was only witnessed by my dinner of biscuits, cheese, apple, and wine.

In my mind, I can hear the prose that would have tripped off your tongue after having witnessed such a sight. You would have been alight with curiosity and praise. I am sure some line from *The Rime of the Ancient Mariner* would have been quoted by you, dear Anne. It is a spice missing in this life of mine, your artful way with words and keen, observing mind.

Yours,
Captain Frederick Wentworth
HMS Asp

Had Frederick been in the library with me, he would have laughed heartily at my expense. For at that moment, the wind buffeted the panes of the window with a ferocity that made me startle. Flecks of ice and branches smacked the glass several times. I could almost imagine a tunnel of wind and snow reaching from the sky to twirl our manor house about and crush it into a pile of dust and brick. Several waterspouts of that size must have been terrifying. I could hardly imagine it, even with the gift of my vivid imagination.

Frederick's cool head had saved the *Asp* and her crew from panic and a grisly fate, not for the first or last time. I wished then that Frederick and our son were there so that I could join them in a merry laugh at my skittish response, for I was sure I jumped enough out of my chair that daylight could be seen.

Dear Anne,

We have taken many ships of privateers, who would have preyed on British commerce in these waters, since arriving here in the West Indies; privateers are little better than their near cousins, pirates. The salient difference is that privateers possess the official sanction of a government to conduct the business of pillaging English interests on the waters. Our own government has issued many letters of marque to shipowners, allowing them to plunder the vessels of our enemies.

Pirates answer to no one. They pillage and murder as they see fit on any ship unlucky enough to cross their paths, regardless of nationality. Pirates face execution, while privateers face imprisonment and the possibility of being traded in a prisoner exchange back to their native country. The distinction between the two is a matter of life and death.

Thus far, we have been fortunate enough in our wanderings through these waters to only encounter privateers with official documentation to back up their claim to legitimate privateering. I am relieved. You know me too well, Anne, to doubt that I will have a heavy heart indeed when the day comes that we take a ship with no letter of marque. None will guess at the turmoil that will roil my heart at the prospect of sending a ship full of men, murderous, vicious men to be sure, to their hanging back at port. I take no pleasure in such a duty that will be required of me. But to my duty, I will always be true to the best of my ability.

As the riches of our captures of French merchants and privateers pile up, the fortunes of some of these good men who serve under me will be made. I include myself in that group. For that I am grateful. I have been fortunate enough to be blessed with an unnaturally adept and intelligent group of officers. Not one of them has been a millstone of incompetence hanging about my neck. Captains have a long history of trying to pawn off the buffoons of officers onto each other. It is a hard thing indeed to witness men of lesser ability and character advance in the profession due to their birth, wealth, and connexions.

Although all my officers have impressed me one way or another over the last few months, there is one that stands out profoundly. He is Lieutenant Benwick, and he, like myself, had little to recommend him beyond his damn fine seamanship and intelligence. Since making so many valuable captures of prize ships, I have had the opportunity to entertain the officers with a few fine dinners in my cabin when we are away from port. I realise it is a very beneficial thing to get to know the lower-ranking officers in a more informal setting and will make us a better crew for it. It is a terrible shame that the Admiralty does not realise the value of this and makes us poorly funded captains buy all of our food out of pocket. It is unwise.

At our last dinner, Benwick opened up a bit and even quoted a few lines of poetry with a fine voice. The wine had loosened his tongue, and I encouraged him to recite some more. My mind drifted to you, Anne, and I had to look down on more than one occasion to disguise the moisture in my eye. You would enjoy meeting him. Dear Anne, I wish to God that you were here to—

Yes, I am fortunate in officers, Benwick especially. He has proved himself to be quick of mind and body, able to understand far-reaching strategies that fly over the heads of most, capable of plotting a course with admirable accuracy and no errors in his arithmetic, and cheerful in fellowship once the right amount of spirits has been plied upon him. Usually, he is a most serious, bookish fellow. I hope I may further his interests in the future. There are several entries in my logbook noting his heroic actions. He is the sort to never mention his own accomplishments, even with a few sheets to the wind, therefore I must do it for him. Were you here—

No, I cannot contain it, Anne. I wish you were here. Every day with all my heart. Staying in Port Charlotte Amalie, waiting for me at each break in our action. Here to tell my tall tales to, counsel me with your wisdom through difficult times, and liven up the gatherings with my officers. The only danger would be the risk of them losing their hearts to you as much as I… and now I forget myself in speculation. 'Tis a dangerous habit when I write these letters. I must be more watchful in the future. It can lead to no good.

Yours,

Captain Frederick Wentworth

HMS Asp

I had always strongly suspected that Frederick never truly stopped caring for me after I had broken off our engagement. Neither of us dwelled much on those miserable few years when we were forced apart. It was a painful time, and every moment we gave over to remembrance of it was a moment we lost to make happy memories for ourselves.

I stood and took the letters in one hand and my candle in the other. I left the soundless library to go upstairs to bed. The house was unusually silent. The snow had finally ceased to fall outside. Everything seemed hushed under the blanket of cold.

As I lay in bed, I reflected on how Frederick had genuinely struggled to overcome his regard for me. He had truly thought himself beyond the binding of our love for each other by the time he returned to England in 1814, eight years after our first engagement and a mere seven years after composing those letters.

I had received a proposal of marriage from another man, Charles Musgrove, but had refused without a moment's hesitation. Frederick had been pursued by Catherine LaCroix in the West Indies. He had engaged the affections of both of the fine young Uppercross ladies when he returned here to England after his adventures at sea. We both had our opportunities to move on from one another. Opportunities with men and women who possessed a higher intelligence than most. We both declined those chances. In our hearts, if not in our minds, we knew the impossibility of life without one another and chose our paths accordingly. No one else would do for either of us. Such kindred spirits were we that time and the distance of half the globe did nothing to dampen our love. I fell under the spell of sleep with my heart warm and a smile on my lips.

CHAPTER SIX

The morning after a snow—was there anything more gloriously beautiful and deadly? A snow crusted over with ice always brought to mind my elder sister, Elizabeth. I was quite sure she would revel in the comparison to indescribable beauty, and perhaps agree with the chilly nature of her heart as well. I thought of her with something like regret on that frigid morning. She was still ensconced in their little kingdom in Bath. How impersonal Bath must have felt, all abandoned streets and hard faces. When Frederick had returned from the seas a wealthy man, I suspected she may have had some designs on him. Elizabeth Elliot of Kellynch could have done much worse than accept a rich naval officer with prospects of becoming an admiral some day and, perhaps, a lord.

Although all who knew our family well would say she had done little to deserve my sympathy, I could not help but think such a cold morning as this must make her reflect on her past and the slim hope of a propitious alliance for an unmarried woman of little fortune and thirty-six years. I sincerely hoped there would be a well-attended concert for her to attend. She loved nothing better than to disregard the music being played and to disparage the fashions of others. Elizabeth rarely left Bath for any cause. She felt keenly the smallness of her position outside of that narrow social circle. Occasionally, she visited our very wealthy, distant cousins, the Dalrymples, as she had succeeded in eventually edging her way into their good graces. It must have elevated her spirits to walk among such lofty halls as they possessed. I genuinely hoped it did her good.

As I lay there contemplating the snow and my sister, Maude came in to open the curtains and set a breakfast tray on the table beside me.

"Goodness, Maude! It is unlike me to stay in bed until this hour, is it not? Thank you for your thoughtfulness."

"My pleasure, ma'am. Both Betsy and I noticed you stayed up late with your readings. If you don't mind my saying so, if I may be so bold—"

"Being bold has rarely stopped you from speaking up in the past, Maude. I hope you feel free to share what needs my attention."

"You are all goodness, ma'am. Many were the times I angered those I worked for. I once had a lady throw her slipper at my head for pointing out that another lady was planning to wear the exact same gown as she to a grand ball! I never heard a thank you, even though I'm sure I saved her from some embarrassment. Imagine, I thought she would be grateful, ma'am. I'll not say the name of the lady, ma'am, out of respect."

"Very wise, as always," I murmured as I poured myself a cup of tea. "You were about to say something...bold?"

"Oh, yes! Betsy and I were remarking that you look a bit tired these days, ma'am. I think you ought not to stay up so late, reading your books. I can bring you breakfast every morning till you get the strength of your blood back up."

My palm cradled my cheek. I had suspected the truth of what she was saying for a few weeks. Some ladies may have been furious, but I was secretly grateful for the confirmation of my suspicions.

"You should probably not venture such words to ladies in the future, Maude." I reached my hand to touch her forearm. "But it is much appreciated in this instance."

Maude blushed and turned to finish straightening the curtains before hurrying out of the room. I said a silent thank you for my bold, meddlesome, caring, loyal servants. One was not always so fortunate to encounter a Betsy, Maude, or Jim. Others must have wondered as to why, with Frederick's fortune, we lived in a small manor house below our means. I had always noticed that the smaller the manor, the more of a family atmosphere could be nurtured by the inhabitants. My history of being a captain's wife and daughter of a baronet had included a wide variety of living situations. I had managed everything from a snug, one-room cabin aboard a ship of men, to grand manor houses in foreign ports. My contentment seemed to be most steady in a happy medium between the two. Our house was just grand enough to satisfy society as to the manner in which a wealthy captain should live and cosy enough for the fulfilment of those who craved simpler pleasures.

Feeling refreshed from my tea and toast, I picked up the next letter in Frederick's unsent correspondence.

Dearest Anne,

Do you recall during one of our first encounters, we were deep in conversation off to the side of some room, and you enquired whether I spoke French? I laugh at the memory myself.

'Of course!' I answered, brimming with confidence and hoping to impress the most beautiful, accomplished woman I had ever laid eyes on. I failed, of course, to mention the level of my fluency, which, I gathered by the twinkle of your eye, you were curious to test. You then recited a tangle of poetry that I could barely decipher. I felt like a man treading water hoping to grasp a floating bit of lumber!

'That has always been one of my favourites. What is your opinion on how the poet expressed himself, sir?' you asked in that gentle but firm voice of yours.

'Well, I thought he spoke most eloquently on the beauty and majesty of...the teeth of his favourite horse?'

The rest of the folks gathered looked with keen interest at the burst of laughter that followed from both of us. You always knew how to spot a ruse from me, Anne.

I am happy to inform you that I have one aboard my ship who could rival your capacity at foreign tongues. Lieutenant Benwick, as First Lieutenant Conner has informed me, speaks four languages well. His father is a highly educated clergyman of limited means. I called Benwick to my cabin. Through his disguise of an expressionless face, I sensed he was nervous at this mysterious summons from his captain.

'Ah, Benwick, I see we have caught you before your morning shave, excellent. I've been informed by Conner that you have some skill in speaking other languages. Is this true?'

'Yes, sir. I speak French, Spanish, Italian, but only a bit of German.'

'I see. I've been thinking of conducting a reconnaissance mission for information as to where we may locate a certain ship. You, of course, know we have taken almost a dozen privateers and several French merchant ships since we arrived here almost a year ago. It has come to my attention that one pirate ship in particular has done brisk business in capturing ships and slaughtering all on board. Just about a week ago, the northern coast of the island saw an American ship by the name of *Mercury* drift upon shore, ransacked and deserted. I think we can presume all aboard are dead.

There have been several English ships that are unaccounted for in the region, and we must presume this particular pirate ship, the *Dire Fortune*, is to blame. Her captain is an Englishman by the name of Jebediah Twist. Rumour is that he has some bit of education and cleverness about him, which makes him all the more of a dangerous foe. I have no way of knowing if he is on *Dire Fortune* or one of his other, smaller vessels, but so many deaths are connected to that particular man that a show of English naval strength is needed to save the lives of every nation. We must try and discover her whereabouts.'

'Yes, sir.'

'To that end, I propose that we sail the *Asp* to the northern shore under the cover of darkness, and we set anchor off of Picara Point. You and I will row a boat ashore, visit the tavern there, the Black Orchid, and see what we might uncover. Understood?'

'Yes, sir.'

'Benwick, this mission is unofficial and voluntary. If you do not wish to participate, you need not.'

'I wish to be included, sir.'

'Excellent, for if we had to rely on my ability to translate other languages, we may well have ended up aground off the coast of Greenland. Only you and Conner are familiar with the details of our trip to the tavern, but I suspect the rest of the crew will easily guess at least part of what we do. Now, see Conner for some clothing that will aid us in blending in with the locals and be prepared to leave tonight. You have the rest of the day off to sleep and eat as you see fit in order to be at full alertness for our nighttime mission.'

Benwick saluted and turned to leave. To sleep? Probably not. As a young officer of nineteen years, I doubt he could have slept a wink with the prospect of such an adventure in the near future.

That evening, the two of us set forth to row our way to shore from the *Asp*. We had the help of two additional seamen to aid us with the rowing, but it was tough going for me, as it had been years since I laid my hand to an oar.

Once ashore, the men who accompanied us took to the brush with the boat while Benwick and I made our way along the beach to the Black Orchid tavern. I, in my tattered clothes and a dirty kerchief tied tight round my head, would have made a fine spectacle for your family to comment on had they been witness.

We entered the inn and took two spots at the bar to lean on and order rum. As the evening progressed and the noise increased, we began to circulate, hoping our quest for knowledge of the *Dire Fortune* would be unremarkable to the rest of the patrons. I was pleased to see with what ease Benwick made the rounds, conversing effortlessly in many languages with the rummiest of bounders there. I had advised him to approach the evening with the same spirit he used when giving recitations of poetry. To imagine himself as one of these gents and truly believe himself a part of a pirate crew, from the ragged kerchief on his head to the dirt beneath his nails. I think you would have been proud of our portrayal, Anne.

Benwick came up to me and gave me a small nudge on my elbow. Apparently, he had obtained some hints as to where we would have the best chances of finding the *Dire Fortune*. We finished our drinks and headed out into the night and back down towards the beach.

'Sir, I believe we picked up some followers,' Benwick muttered.

Without looking all the way round, out of the corner of my eye, I perceived movement in the under-growth behind us.

'Let them believe they have the element of surprise. Keep moving ahead,' I whispered.

I had a pistol stowed under my baggy shirt and bulky vest in the back of my trousers, as did Benwick. But we both knew that the pistols being shot should be the last resort so that we could avoid drawing unwanted attention. Whether these scoundrels were informants for the *Dire Fortune*, or they were fortune seekers who had noticed a slight jingle of coins in our purses, I know not. For at that moment, just as we were in sight of our boat stored under the trees, they sprang.

We had barely heard the cutthroats approach, as this must be a regular habit for them, and had just turned round with our dirk knives drawn when they sprang on us. A chaotic battle ensued, and at one point there was a scramble for my pistol that had tumbled loose.

The two seamen left to guard the rowboat had

come up to assist at that point, but all was over and done. The scoundrels were dead, those few seconds of cognisance of their approach being our salvation. Benwick and I, covered in blood, dirty from the battle, dragged the bodies towards the trees without delay. A shallow grave was dug for each, and they were buried with a few palm branches scattered about to disguise their final resting place. They will be discovered, but not, hopefully, for a few days. By then, we will be far away and too close to our quarry, the *Dire Fortune*, to be stopped by any intelligence those two may have provided.

By pretending to seek to become a member of the pirate ship's crew, Benwick discovered its last known course. He could not uncover with any certainty whether Captain Twist was aboard her or not. Time will tell, if our luck holds. I hope to God that the intelligence will aid us in finding the ship and saving countless lives.

Yours, dear Anne,

Captain Frederick Wentworth

HMS Asp

The letter lowered to my lap. A sudden crossness tightened my chest. Foolish Frederick! How had he not found another able officer to go ashore and worm out confidences among the Black Orchid's patrons? His middling skills in French gave him little advantage in a tavern that must have been filled to the rafters with every language of the globe. Better to send one of the officers who excelled in combat, or better yet, one of the hale and hearty seamen who had iron and blood in his veins and looked the part. Why risk the life of the captain on such an errand?

The answer slowly crept on me, and it left a sour taste in my mouth. Was he seeking out danger to escape thoughts of me? Thoughts of our broken engagement? Had not Benwick's sharp eye perceived the cutthroats following them along that lonely beach, it could have been Frederick whose last resting place was under the palms of St Thomas.

I rubbed my hand across my forehead and fought off a rising queasiness. Those scars that lined his back, that I had felt beneath my fingertips just a few nights before—how many were from heedless risks that could be traced to Frederick's quest to mend a broken heart? Those scars, how many were of my own making?

I rose from bed and dressed myself quickly. The movement went some way in settling my uneasiness. I knew there were several correspondences on my writing desk that I had been neglecting ever since the discovery of the trunk in the attic. Had the weather been more inviting, I would have taken a walk out in our small park to clear my head and settle my heart. But the heavy snow, followed by a bitterly cold night, was now in the sloppy process of being vanquished by a turn of warming sunshine.

CHAPTER SEVEN

Later, I looked up from my desk, my hand holding a pen arrested in midair, to see a sludge of watery ice slide with a thumping crash from the roof and onto the ground. I shook my head with a wry grin. Frederick and Freddie's trip would be even more lengthened. The muddy roads would be just as impassable had they been coated in icy snow.

It was for the best, I supposed. I knew their presence would be a tonic of cheerful noisiness to Kellynch Hall. I looked back at the heavy work of writing my elder sister Elizabeth, who had formerly presided over Kellynch with regal stoicism. The poor financial management of both my father and Elizabeth had resulted in the renting of Kellynch to Admiral and Mrs Croft and their relocating to Bath. Although my heart mourned the loss of my childhood home, I thought that it was perhaps a change for the better. The current residents were better stewards of the place, the surrounding crofters, and all of its beauties.

I returned to the wearisome task at hand, keeping up an

unrewarding exchange of letters with Elizabeth. Her information of Bath was detached and selected carefully to make herself and Father appear in only the very best light. At least letters from my younger sister, Mrs Mary Musgrove, were full of pert and sometimes funny complaints and gossip. She even occasionally remembered to enquire as to my welfare, that was then followed by a demand for a visit from me as soon as possible.

Finally finishing the letter to Elizabeth made me lean my head back, close my eyes, and sigh. Maude entered to inform me of lunch being served.

"Here now, ma'am. Have you gone and worn yourself out? Betsy made some of those parsnips just the way you like."

"Thank you, Maude. I shall be there directly. I have just finished a letter to my sister...Miss Elliot."

Maude nodded knowingly, pressing her lips tight to keep from saying something she ought not. The letters from Frederick confirmed what I had long believed. The local families did not hold my father and older sister in high esteem. Heaven only knew what Maude and Betsy might have heard of them. I could not have said much in defence of my family.

"Yes, ma'am. I'll let Betsy know to brew the tea extra strong today."

She exited in a flurry. I took my packet of letters and left for lunch and the next chapter in my dear Frederick's escapades.

My Dearest Anne,

The *Dire Fortune* was within our reach. We had played a game of cat and mouse with her for the last several weeks just to the east of the Bahamas Islands. It seems fitting that we finally saw her floundering in the weak wind off the east coast of Cat Island. Her progress was slow as she fought to stay off the leeward shore of Cat Island and make some headway back out towards the open sea. No doubt she had gone close to the shore in the hopes of eluding us in some cove or inlet for a day. Perhaps they were trying to lead us into waters where we were sure to be grounded.

The poor wind was making slow work of it. We had the advantage of catching that bit of wind and making our way to her from the open sea while avoiding any dangerous shoals. The bad luck of it was that the *Dire Fortune* had plenty of time to prepare, since we had been in view for quite a while. We had to be on our toes, knowing there could be some well-laid trap awaiting us. I ordered an early lunch for the men, anticipating that dinner may never come today. We were half a league away when I ordered the boatswain to pipe to quarters (being too small a ship for a drummer, he pipes the men to their stations).

Anne, it was a long, slow slog. The pirates fought for their lives, outlasting the men of a privateer ship by far. They knew the end of this battle would only hold a hangman's noose for them. The wind was barely moving, and both ships fired upon each other through a heavy, heated cloud of smoke. Our more disciplined, diligent training won out at last. The constant drilling to reduce the amount of time between firing and reloading was what won us the battle, as usual. Our volleys were relentless and precise.

The *Dire Fortune* got in their fair share of good shots as well. I was standing on deck, just turned from the enemy ship to convey instructions to First Lieutenant Conner when the nearby balustrade was shattered into bits by a cannonball. My back received a blistering of hot, sharp shards of wood. Had I been facing forward, I may have lost my life. I felt large splinters in my flesh, stinging. Warm blood ran down my face. Conner turned white as a sheet and attempted to steer me towards the doctor below deck.

'Belay that, Conner. I will not leave the deck till I see this through to the end. A few little splinters need not stop me.'

I can see you shaking your head at me, Anne. I was, perhaps, being bullheaded. I know it is one of the qualities in me you most admire. Or detest. I could never make out your exact feelings on that point. The battle was near over, as we had de-masted the *Dire Fortune* and our seamen and marines were already on its deck, fighting through the tangle of bodies, rigging, sails, and fallen masts.

When all appeared well in hand, the few remaining pirates still alive were brought aboard the *Asp* and lined up with their hands tied behind their backs. I walked up and down the line slowly, examining each face closely. Perhaps somewhere in this group, Captain Twist was hidden. It would have been a clever move to blend among the men and elude detection. Had I been a pirate, I would have done that very thing.

I closely observed the ears of each. They keep some of their fortune on them in the form of gold rings pierced through the skin of their ears. The wealthier the man, the greater the number of loops of gold. I could discern no great quantity of gold on any one man.

Blood trickled freely down my back, and I began to feel the weariness of the past several hours of heat, smoke, and noise. I turned to Conner and Benwick.

'Conner, see that the prisoners are turned out of

their clothes and washed thoroughly of vermin and lice. Shave their heads as well. Their injuries are to be tended to, and then a meal. Benwick, you are unharmed as well? Good, get over to the *Dire Fortune*, make sure the marines are stationed outside the magazine, organise the cleaning of the deck, cut away sails that are unsalvageable, and have the carpenter get her masted again.'

I stepped closer to avoid being overheard by the prisoners. 'And gentlemen, pay close attention to the bodies of the dead, notice if any of their earlobes look recently torn and bloodied. It could be that Captain Twist removed his gold rings before battle. I doubt any of this rummy lot of prisoners will tell who or where Twist is.'

I straightened my spine and walked with my hands clasped behind my back all the way to my cabin. Once inside with the door shut, I collapsed in a chair and began the excruciating process of trying to remove my jacket. I stifled a yell. As some of the splinters were so large, they had my jacket pinned to me.

Fortunately, my man Owen came in, saw the dilemma I was in, and began to cut away my jacket with scissors he kept for repairs to my uniform. I grumbled at poor Owen terribly for ruining my perfectly good uniform. He bore it silently, good man, knowing it was pain and exhaustion speaking. Once the jacket and shirt were off, he fetched the doctor from his work below to pull and clean my back of wood. It was a painful business, I have no shame in telling you, Anne, and I sought the support of rum to dull my senses.

It was an eventful few days, and now we are on our way back to Port Charlotte Amalie to complete the remaining repairs to the *Asp* and *Dire Fortune*. It is a fine prize ship that contains some of Twist's treasures, although but a fraction of what he probably actually possesses. It is probable that the *Dire Fortune* is just one of many ships of a fleet that he lords over. It is difficult to get any truly reliable intelligence about the pirates in these waters.

I am on the way to being healed. The doctor says I shall have a pretty map of scars upon my back for the rest of my days. But since I am unable to witness them with my own eyes, why should I care?

Yours truly,

Captain Frederick Wentworth

HMS Asp

I sat at the table long past when the dishes had been cleared away. Only a solitary cup of cold tea remained on the table-cloth to greet that last, heartrending letter as I set it down.

What if Frederick Wentworth had not returned and offered his hand in marriage a second time? What if the eight years we were separated after our broken engagement had truly and completely quelled his love for me? Would there have been enough courage in my breast to forge my own path? Perhaps. Or perhaps I would have succumbed to family influences again and allowed myself to be steered into a loveless marriage with my cousin Mr Elliot.

But I had chosen, regardless of any judgment of family and friends, to engage myself to Frederick for a second and final time. I had no care for their approval. Only our happiness mattered.

I stood, breathing deeply the air around me. The scents of

our home on land. The knowledge that I had nothing to regret of the path that I was on. It was a contentment that I felt down to my bones. It had nothing to do with the manor house we inhabited or the fortune Frederick had accumulated through prize money. It was the certainty that Frederick and I had an entwined destiny. Even if that destiny found me setting up house in a foreign land at any time, we would find our happiness together.

I had a private smile at the thought of Maude, fussing with local vendors in some exotic land for the best quality of cheese at the best price. When one had a large household, the destinies of many were meshed with yours.

CHAPTER EIGHT

I forbade myself from reading an additional letter for the
rest of the day. The pile of remaining missives had
grown thin, and I wanted to savour what was left for me
to read. I had finally convinced Maude to accompany me
back up to the attic for an additional sorting of belongings
that had become far too haphazard for the high standards of
a captain's wife.

The weariness I felt that evening as I crawled into bed
surprised me. It had been a long afternoon of shoving
trunks, reviewing their contents, and sorting them out. My
time left to do such a task without the 'helpful hands' of little
Freddie was waning. I imagined that after a sunny day full of
a drying wind, they would attempt to forge their way back
home tomorrow. I was sure to be greeted by muddy hugs,
red noses, and tales of adventure. My heart cheered at the
image.

Although sleepiness and the warmth of my bed tugged at
me to lie down, I had to read more. I broke the seal on the
next letter.

My Dearest Anne,

Port Charlotte Amalie is abuzz with our battle with the *Dire Fortune*. The only dark cloud to lessen the praise is the fact that we cannot make out whether Captain Twist was among the dead. I begin to doubt it. His men will not turn on him; I do admire their loyalty.

People who claim to have seen him do not think he was among the living or dead that we have described. That is a murky source of facts, though. These pirates sprout legends and tall tales around them like so many barnacles on the hull of a ship. It would take a man with more patience than I to scrape through the thousands of false tales to find one pearl of truth. You know me well enough, Anne; I have no gift for such things.

Our orders were waiting for us upon our return. The *Asp* is to sail back to England within the week. I am to be given command of the frigate HMS *Laconia*. It is likely to be the last big voyage of the dear, old *Asp*. She was only certified for home service a year ago, but the Admiralty deemed her fit enough to carry almost one hundred men across the Atlantic. She has done that and more.

I am so thankful to have had the chance to sail her. I am thankful to her for seeing me through very dark days from which I thought I may never recover. She saw me enter a pauper and leave a man of fortune. The merchant and privateer ships we took with her and the prize money we made has left all of us wealthier than we were a year ago.

The officers and I attended one last ball at the LaCroix manor given in our honour. It was a magnificent affair, and I spent much of the time trying my best to elude the persistent Catherine LaCroix. She valiantly attempted to corner me for the purpose of wrenching moments of sighs and promises. She was even so bold in the pressing of her suit that she reached out and touched the top of my hand with her fingertips when she was unobserved by anyone else. I was shocked. But it was not a shock of passion, as Miss LaCroix had most likely intended. It was the shock of remembrance. The only thing I yearned for in that moment was to relive that precious evening when I proposed marriage to you almost a year in the past.

Do you remember, Anne? We stood close, listening to a young girl from my brother's parish bang away at that poor pianoforte with an abundance of gusto and little talent. A piece by Joseph Haydn, if memory serves, in the key of C. If only that young woman had been aware of the powerful effect her terrible performance had on me. I was compelled to a moment of improper boldness. I touched my fingers onto the inside of your wrist and softly slid them down to the palm of your hand. You did not draw away. You stood perfectly still. And then, to my heart's forever joy, your little fingers curled up around mine, and pressed them close.

Oh, how I wish that caterwauling tune had never stopped. I could have stood there forever, in all the warmth of love, a bubble, only the two of us in the entire world. But the song ended. As I helped you with your jacket, I murmured my proposal in the dark entryway, away from prying eyes, into your delicate ear. You looked up.

'Yes' was your only response.

Those eyes of yours were on fire with the nearness of our bodies. I remember you reached and clasped my hands with yours for a brief moment, before the noise of others approaching caused us to break apart. But, I get carried away. I am glad, really, that you will never see these pages. It lends a certain freedom to my pen that I would never dare venture otherwise. I would give anything to return to those happy few hours, before the rest of the world pressed in on all sides to prune our courtship down to a withered stub.

I could curse myself for not demanding you accompany me at once to Gretna Green for an elopement. That night. Immediately after hearing your 'yes' spoken aloud. I often ponder whether, in the heat of that moment, after the wretched piano performance and our brief meeting in the hall, you would have willingly agreed to an elopement. If I might have grabbed your hand and pulled you into the nearest carriage and ordered the driver to whip the horses to top speed and not stop till we were safely away to our elopement, would you have agreed? Remembering the look in your eyes that night, I think there is some small chance that you would have.

I will never know, fool that I am. I lacked the courage with you that I had gladly displayed in battle with a French ship of the line, outgunned by a hundred cannons and a thousand men.

But I lose the thread of my thoughts, as I often do when pondering different paths I might have taken with you, Anne. Miss Catherine LaCroix looked chagrined at my rebuff, but I believe a woman of her temperament will not long suffer from despair over the loss of me. I wish her better luck at finding more malleable material on the next English ship that arrives.

Thoughts of returning to England leave me with a

mix of joy and trepidation. I will be genuinely happy to see my sister and brother again, if I have time before we receive our next orders. My brother is in a new parish, so there is little chance that you and I will meet again at his old one in Somersetshire. I suppose that is for the best.

Even now with my growing fortune, I have no certainty that I would meet with approval from your family or friends. If one of the prize ships had earned me a title as well, then maybe. But no matter how wealthy I may become, I shall always be just a sailor from a family with no title. Here, you see the famous courage of 'Steely Went' falter. I shall not risk it. My heart, torn asunder once, barely stitched back together after almost a year at sea, could not survive if you were to reject me a second time. I would die. I cannot risk it, ever, even for your sake, dearest Anne. Forgive me for my cowardice.

Ever Yours,

Captain Frederick Wentworth

HMS Asp

I heard a fox call in the milky night beyond my window. Much of the snow had melted during the day. There was enough left to give the night an eerie glow here and there. I knew by the hush of the house that it must be late. What would I have done? Had Frederick swept me into a carriage and raced me to Gretna Green for an elopement, would I have melted to his iron will and abandoned all? Would I have drawn close to him in the carriage and kissed his lips a thousand times? We would have suffered. Perhaps my father would have meddled in a way to ruin Frederick's career. I would not put it past him. But when I reflected on the eight years both Frederick and I suffered from low spirits and a broken heart, which would have been worse? If I could go back to advise that young woman in the darkened hall, her ears still ringing from the abuse the pianoforte suffered, her hand still burning from her sweetheart's forbidden touch, I would whisper into her ear to fly as quick as a sparrow towards happiness and an uncertain future. Be with the one you love, no matter the cost.

I could not resist another of those letters that caused me so many tears and so much laughter. My hand reached over and took hold of a rather thick letter that had required a bit more sealing wax than the rest.

My Dearest Anne,

Like a habit whose temptation I cannot resist, I pick up my pen again to talk to you through ink and paper. It is a poor substitute, but one that must serve.

We were but two days into our voyage home when we saw a ship in the distance, listing to one side, the telltale signs of being incommoded by a leak in her hull. They must have been working the pumps furiously to stay afloat. It did not look good. It was a frigate of about twenty-eight guns, but so badly in need of assistance that I thought only of assisting the crew as best we could.

To be cautious, we came up on the port side of the ship. It was leaning most towards the water, rendering the guns on that side almost useless. She flew no colours, and there was little sign of activity on deck. I could spy very well some coverings on the deck as we drew near. I turned to Conner.

'I don't like it. Feels like a trap. Tell the boatswain to get the men to their guns below deck using words, no pipe. We don't want to give away to this ship that we are ready for battle. Tell them to grease the wheels of the cannons and lay down some burlap so they squeak less rolling up into place. Leave the gunports closed. Stay at the hatch to yell down the orders to fire.'

'Could be a plague ship, sir. Perhaps there are bodies under those tarpaulins, sir.'

'Could be, Lieutenant Conner, but my stomach is telling me a trap, not the plague.'

'Yes, sir.'

I took my hailing trumpet and called to the listing ship. 'If you are in need of assistance, please stand by. Is there illness aboard?'

As I suspected, the tarpaulins flew off and a row of cannons, brought up to the deck from the port side below, were armed and ready. I signalled to Conner; he shouted below. Our starboard side gunports flew open, and we shot off a first volley several seconds before them. Our few marines scurried into the rigging to open fire from above onto their decks.

The men we fought had more the look of pirates than privateers. It was hardscrabble to be sure, but we brought off victory in a short time. The ship was bigger, with more guns, but whatever damage there was to her hull below the waterline made it quick work for us to beat her. A few shots from our half dozen volleys had her dismasted. We had fired grapeshot as well to do as much damage to the men on deck as possible. By this time, I was certain they were pirates and would fight fiercely. The ship listed even more now, taking on additional water, as we may have increased the damage below the waterline. The pumps that had been working hard getting water out of the ship were most likely unmanned, and the water was flowing in freely. If we could get aboard and assess the damage quickly, there was a chance she was still salvageable. We hooked lines of rope onto her using grapples and dragged the ship close to us so that we could get aboard and finish off the few remaining fighters. Conner came up to me, covered in the smoke and grime of the guns below deck. Once we had our injured below to see the doctor, Conner and I went to the other ship to glean some knowledge of this dubious vessel.

'It is called the *Preston Bones*, another ship belonging to Jebediah Twist,' Conner informed me.

'Is Captain Twist aboard?'

Before he could reply, I saw a dreaded tendril of smoke from below at the stern.

'Did you post guards at the magazine?' I demanded of Conner. But I knew my answer in his dawning look of horror. I had given the order before we boarded, and he must have neglected that duty. If my ship were sinking, to cause chaos and destroy as many of the enemy as possible, I would have set the magazine on fire as well. That tiny room full of barrels of black gunpowder would blow us all to hell.

'Abandon ship!' I cried, waving my men back to the *Asp*. Something behind me exploded. The world around me went dark.

The next thing I knew, I was waking up aboard the *Asp* and Benwick was shouting for men to get me below deck to the doctor. I lost my grasp on consciousness again.

I awoke in my cabin, lying on my side on a pallet on the floor. My lower back hurt terribly. I was quite tied up around the waist with a thick swath of bandaging. The explosion must have caused me a very grave injury. Benwick came in.

'The *Preston Bones* burst apart and sank, sir. Conner was killed.'

My heart wrenched in pain, adding to my misery. 'You are acting first lieutenant, Benwick. Hand me the ship's log, if you please. I wish to make an official note that you have charge of the ship while I am injured.'

'Sir, the doctor says—'

'Damn the doctor and hand me the ship's log. As soon as we are able, set course back to Charlotte Amalie. I will not have these cutthroat prisoners aboard us all the way across the Atlantic, eating all our provisions and plotting murder, just to hang by their neck in England.'

'Yes, sir.'

'And Benwick, who pulled me off the burning *Preston Bones?*'

'I did, sir.'

'I see, saved your captain from an early appointment in Davy Jones's locker, eh? Thank you, Benwick. You'll need to see to Conner's funeral as well. It seems that I am unable to move about much at the moment.'

Anne, so ends a year of wealth, heartache, and adventure. I lost Conner, for which I am deeply saddened. I will make no mention in the ship's log of his lapse in duty that cost us the *Preston Bones* and his life. I have no way of knowing whether the fire was set and out of control before we boarded, or if Conner's negligence caused the explosion by allowing the pirates time to set the magazine aflame. There was a chance the *Preston Bones* may have been unsalvageable anyway, as its hull was taking on water rapidly. I will not condemn the man to professional shame or cause his family more misery. Therefore, I will list the probable cause of the fire as attempts of the pirates to sabotage their own vessel before we boarded.

I have gained a most excellent acting first lieutenant in Benwick. I will do what I can to further his career and request that he accompany me onto the HMS *Laconia*. My life is in his debt, and I hope that I may one day be of service to him as deeply as he has been to me.

Yours, Forever and Entirely,
Captain Frederick Wentworth
HMS Asp

Perhaps it was the lateness of the hour or from overexertion in the attic that day, but my head swam. How many times had I come close to losing my Frederick forever? Through the violence of nature, man, or chance? I did not want to know. Sleep overcame me as I still pressed Frederick's letter to my chest, tears rolling down my cheeks.

CHAPTER NINE

I awoke the next morning, late, to another brilliant day. The sun shone, and I knew in my heart that Frederick and our son would brave the mud to voyage home. I was glad they had been able to spend a few extra nights at the Crofts'. Time on land was so precious to the men of His Majesty's Navy. I never knew when our time together may end and Frederick would be called upon to serve in his capacity as a captain.

Things were changing rapidly. Bonaparte was no longer a threat, and France appeared settled at the moment. There were few in the world who wished to engage the undeniably dominant British Royal Navy. Frederick had been at the launching of the first steam-powered boat, the HMS *Comet*, at the end of May. Even though it was just to be utilised as a tug in the Thames, Frederick said he knew this to be a portend of things to come. The navy our son would see in his life would be a very different sort of beast.

These thoughts stewed in my mind as I pushed up to sitting. Once again, Maude had thoughtfully brought breakfast up to me. I looked to the last letter of the pile. It had its seal intact. It was thin, and I smiled at the thought of Frederick unable to resist one last note to me. Had I started down such a road of correspondence as he, it would have been difficult to resist picking up the pen at every turn of events.

My Dearest Anne,

I am fully healed after a slow but uneventful journey across the Atlantic. The skin of my back is still itchy and stiff, but fully mended with a mighty scar that will show for life. A brief bout of fever after the first few days was the most worrisome part of the injury. Benwick has proved himself above and beyond merely able to run the ship during my convalescence. He will make an admirable captain one day.

We just made it into the sound off Plymouth before a gale of momentous power began to blow. You may notice my writing is not as smooth as usual. That was not intended as a joke. I hear your laugh over the wail of the wind. My writing, even on the calmest days on land, was chicken scratch in your opinion. I will refrain from telling my dear Theresa, for she may take it as a slight to chickens everywhere.

So we are home to England at last, dear Anne, only to be met by the most vicious winds and rain we have ever encountered while on the *Asp*. Even the West Indies treated us to more clement weather than this. It is so foul that we have not been able to leave the *Asp*, although we have been anchored in the harbour for the past two days, well within sight of Plymouth.

Had we been a mere twelve hours later in our arrival, I have no doubt that the *Asp* would be at the bottom of the sea and all of us dead. No amount of skill as a captain could have saved us from a storm such as this on a ship as old as the *Asp*. It would have been a rummy end for us indeed to have survived twice across the Atlantic, more than a dozen battles with privateers and pirates who often outgunned us, to then end so violently within a stone's throw of Plymouth.

It looks as if we may not leave *Asp* for a few days more, as there is no sign of abatement in the weather. It is perhaps as well, Anne, that I was not able to row to shore immediately upon arrival. I may not have prevented myself from riding hard for two days to Kellynch Hall, beating down the doors and insisting that you marry me that very instant. But, time on this heaving sloop with little to do and all the accompanying nausea that even the most seasoned among us are experiencing, has had the result of calming those fires of passion. It has forced me to think with a cooler head that perhaps you have already married another. Or you have no wish of resuming our relationship at all. Worse yet, perhaps you detest me for not fighting harder for you. That is the thought that pains me the most.

These letters, Anne. They started in anger and resentment. Then they became my best companions. My only solace. Now, I must have the strength to put them away forever. I must, or I will not survive. My new life on the HMS *Laconia* awaits. To be always remembering you, thinking of you, telling you of my days, it is a heavy burden that I must attempt to put down so that I may walk tall once again. I will never stop loving you. Every woman I meet is placed next to the paragon of Miss Anne Elliot and found wanting. But perhaps, one day, I will find a lady with enough liveliness, beauty, and wit to make me content. I have a perfect spot in which these letters can slumber, undisturbed, never to be read by me again. I should destroy them completely, but here you see me again shrink away from the thought. To lose this one last thing of you forever, no, I cannot do it. For a second time, we part. A year ago, our parting filled me with rage and thoughts of doing myself some sort of harm. This time, I am filled with doubt as to what might have been and a most pernicious melancholy. In another year, perchance, I shall be fully healed from the wound of separation from you, dear Anne. Goodbye. God bless you.

Yours, Forever and Entirely,
Captain Frederick Wentworth
HMS Asp

And just like that, the door into my Frederick's heart at that time in his life shut tight. I was not at all prepared for how despondent it made me feel. I sifted through the stack of letters, making sure the seal had been broken on each, looking at the dates to be absolutely certain that I had not missed one of the precious missives. But no, all the seals were jagged and broken.

I looked at the date of the very last letter to be certain that I was thinking correctly on it. It was indeed a year to the day when Frederick first proposed to me when he began that last letter in the throes of a tempest in the Plymouth harbour. I closed my eyes, imagining Frederick's tall, muscled frame pacing the interior of the *Asp*'s small, cramped cabin. He would have had to have a perpetual stoop to save his head from constantly being struck on the beams of the ceiling. Had that storm not blown up on him so suddenly, he very well may have begun to travel that very moment to Kellynch to renew his petition for my hand in marriage. But the time and weather made him rethink his passion. So many obstacles by man and nature thrown in our path. I realised that our loving marriage had bonds even stronger because of it. There were even more impediments than I had ever imagined.

Suddenly, I longed to hear his voice and embrace him tightly. As if the universe knew that our love was not to be toyed with any longer, I heard the sounds of muffled boots and squeals of little Freddie downstairs. Maude sounded impatient and worried, just as she ought to be. It was almost midday, and I was still in my nightgown. I stood quickly, but then decided to sit calmly and collect my thoughts. A wave of dizziness descended over me, and I shut my eyes to gather my strength.

The door to the bedroom burst open. The smiling face of my beloved appeared, ruddy from the cold ride. His joy turned to apprehension when he saw me still on the bed.

"Anne, are you well?"

He ran to me and knelt, grasping both my hands in his frozen ones. His brow was knitted in anxiety.

"Your face is pale. Was I that cruel in my letters? Forgive me. I was not myself. I was not myself till you agreed to be my wife years later. We can throw every last one of those blasted letters into the fire right now. I can hardly recall what I wrote in them, I was in such a state of desperation that year. Please, say something!"

I reached my hand to caress his rugged face, smoothing the wrinkles from his brow.

"Where is your crew manifest, my dear?"

He stared back, puzzled.

"Anne, what can you mean?"

I took his hand and placed it on my stomach.

"I have suspected for the last month, but now I am certain. I think it likely you will have an addition to it soon."

A look of wonder replaced all anxiety on Frederick's face. He hugged me tight to him, his face resting on my breast. Then he sat down beside me, giving me several kisses and telling me his joy at the news of a new member to our little crew.

After a few minutes, Frederick stood and walked to the stack of letters on my side of the bed, noting the addition of the ones folded in the shape of ships.

"I trust, then, I was not too offensive? In either set of letters?"

"I have yet to look through the ones from our first engagement, but, no. Not at all. These will join that other precious letter you sent me when you proposed marriage for the second and last time."

"You are correct," he said as he knelt in front of me again, laughing, taking both my hands into his. "It was indeed the second and last proposal, dear Anne."

"And I suppose there are no more stacks of letters written to me that you may have stashed away somewhere secret?"

Frederick grinned that rakish smile of his and stood.

"So, are you telling me that you resisted, for seven more years, putting pen to paper and informing me of all the adventures you experienced while travelling the globe? All the golden-haired governors' daughters you skilfully eluded from their matrimonial snares? There are no more hidden stashes of sealed letters, with my name on them, anywhere in this house?"

Blushing, Frederick said, "I had better go see to our son and how he does with the tea I ordered from the galley."

"Frederick, you never answered my questions!" I stated to

his retreating back as he left our bedroom and descended the stairs, singing a sailor's song at full volume and humming through any inappropriate words for the sake of this house full of ladies.

"Frederick? Frederick! You infuriating man!" I cried after him with a broad smile on my face.

CHAPTER TEN

April 1824

I had never professed myself to be a woman of great activity. A quiet, reflective afternoon with strong tea, an engaging book, and the sporadic intervention of intelligent conversation was my idea of a well-spent day. I did enjoy a walk in good weather and, occasionally, a very long walk. My abilities on a horse would be rumoured to be adequate by generous souls who wished to portray me in the most becoming light. Taking all this into consideration, I liked to think of myself as fairly robust, but perhaps not in vigorously good health.

I had surprised myself with how exceedingly well I bore the many nautical miles I had covered aboard ships while at Captain Frederick Wentworth's side. Some ships were so modest that stretching the limbs for a walk took ingenuity and imagination to accomplish. Later in my husband's career, the larger ships that we were posted to gave more ease of movement. Aboard them, it was much more convenient to walk about and 'get the heat up', as Queen Elizabeth used to say. I rarely experienced two days together of feeling ill while aboard a ship. I rather thought the salty air and swelling of the boards beneath my feet had done my constitution more good than harm. A portion of my first pregnancy was spent on board a ship, and I secretly attributed the ease of my confinement with Freddie to that.

But even the most restrictive of circumstances that I had experienced could not have prepared me for my second confinement. I was far along in my expectation of being safely delivered of another fine, strapping Wentworth child. My confinement had begun early due to the apothecary's concerns about some of my symptoms. Even Maude, that fountain of knowledge on motherhood, advised me to take his instructions to heart. And when Maude agreed with Mr Falgarth, it was an omen that should not be ignored, for she had a decided aversion to medical professionals.

The restrictions to my movements had left me restless. I got up and about as much as was permitted, but it had been a trial on my patience. Although Frederick had stepped up admirably in the running of the house and supervision of his son, I truly missed being about my manor house and supervising the managing of it.

I had just succeeded in sneaking out of bed and stationing myself at the window to admire the frosty morning when I heard the unmistakable sound of pounding hooves coming from across the valley. The road, once it reached our small manor, meandered on for about a half a mile to some fields, then dissipated to nothing at the edge of a small river. That was why the rider I watched with my keenest weather eye struck a chord of dread in my breast. His only destination could be our house. And, in my personal experience, no one with good news rode that swiftly.

I heard the front door open and the message being delivered. By the time he was galloping away, I had made my way to the top of the stairs. Frederick stood below, reading the letter with a serious expression. He must have read it over more than once, because he did not move for a few minutes. Then he turned his head and looked up at me, as if knowing that I was observing him closely. His eye met mine and held it. Then, as per his sometimes-capricious manner, he bounded up the stairs two by two with a bellow that rang through the house.

"What's this? A terrible mutiny if I ever saw one! Left your moorings in the safety of harbour without proper permission? Mr Falgarth will have to be informed of this breach of direct orders. How shall I punish you?"

His smiling face bent over mine for the gentlest of kisses to my cheek when he reached the landing.

"Here now, I will toss you a line and tow you in," he said as he looped my arm through his and steered me back to our bedroom.

Laughing, I replied, "I am not so enormous as to require a tugboat of your size to manoeuvre me, am I?"

"You are perfect as always, Anne. In fact, I think we would all be more settled in mind if you were to put on more weight. I remember you being rounder in face when you were confined with little Frederick. It lent a very pleasing aspect to your visage."

"Did it, now?" I asked as I removed my arm from his and headed towards the chair by the window.

"That does not look like a bed to me," Frederick said with a frown. I saw the fine wrinkles alongside his eyes increase. The dusting of white that was scattered among the hairs of his temples gave him an even more distinguished air than his dark, Irish face formerly had.

"I want to watch as you ride away," I said softly.

Silence followed my quiet statement. I could see the

muscles in Frederick's strong jaw work as he recalled the paper he had stuffed in a pocket.

"The Admiralty has posted me to the HMS *Stoic*. She is a ship of the line. Two decker, ninety guns, eight hundred fifty men. I am to leave for Portsmouth as soon as I may manage. I have orders to proceed without delay to Tuskar Rock off the southeast coast of Ireland. There was a wreck."

I recalled well the name of Tuskar Rock. To imagine that one rock had seen the destruction of so many men and ships, it was unfathomable. Dozens of wrecks on that barren little stretch of rock along St George's Channel. A shudder ran along my spine at the thought of my Frederick in those treacherous waters of the Irish Sea. The tides and wind were unforgiving, and even the most experienced captains sometimes found themselves in danger.

"But, there is a lighthouse there for several years now to prevent such occurrences, is there not?"

"Yes, a lighthouse to warn of the rock during the night, but when the wind comes up and blows you onto its lee shore, the lighthouse will do you little good by night or day. Only two of the crew were lost. But the ship, HMS *Bellona*, is aground, and they want an experienced captain on hand to supervise her being refloated and taken into Wexford. The navy will not want the loss of a three decker like her to those rocks."

Frederick knelt before me and looked up into my face. The anxiety sketched on his made my heart fit to burst. I placed my palm to his cheek.

"I shall fare well, my love. I feel better now that I am taking my ease," I assured him. "Besides, I have the formidable Maude to supervise everything. She will see to my well-being as well as you would."

"I do not like leaving you at a time like this, Anne. You know I shall be thinking of you every moment."

I made to get up to aid him in his preparations for the unexpected return to sea.

"Belay that, Anne." Frederick stood over me with his captain's look that I knew too well. "No need for you to rush around the house to discover the whereabouts of every stray wool sock of mine. I have already laid by plans for just such an occasion."

"But I am really feeling well enough to—"

Frederick raised his hand to halt me. "Let's not have mutinous talk. Freddie is to go for a visit to my sister Sophia and Admiral Croft at Kellynch until either I return or you are safely past your confinement. They were well-informed of such a possibility. Also, Captain and Mrs Harville are to send their eldest girl here to be a companion and aid in the running of the house. Remember little Claire Harville? She is now a fine girl of seventeen, they tell me, and adept at nursing."

"Claire Harville! Last we met, she was barely up to my elbow. Really, Frederick, you need not make so many plans for my welfare. I can do just fine with—"

"Nothing to it. And I have one more surprise for you."

He disappeared out of the room as I resumed my seat in the chair by the window. Frederick returned, holding a bundle before him.

"You have bullied me relentlessly. And so I relent, as I always do, to you."

He handed me another tied bundle of letters. I gasped in surprise and real pleasure at the treasure that he deposited in my lap, wobbling on the edge of my knees before my swollen belly. He knelt before me again.

"To make sure you will not overexert yourself, my love. Letters from my first year in the HMS *Laconia*, to you. I sincerely apologise for the lateness of their arrival, but your generous heart will forgive me, I am sure."

My mind raced back to the ending lines of the letter he had written to me in his last few stormy days aboard the HMS *Asp*. "But in your last letter, you wrote most solemnly that you would cease writing letters to me that you never meant to post."

He grinned in that sly, mischievous way that so resembled our son. "I am usually so good at keeping my promises, but in this instance, I may have succumbed to breaking the faith. You were a hard habit to deny, Anne."

"Thank you," I whispered as I leant forward to give him a kiss.

The next hour was a blur of shouted instructions, rushed notes to be posted, and steps clomping heavily up and down the stairs. Frederick came into the bedroom for one last kiss to me and left in our gig. I watched them wind down our road and then as they progressed across the valley.

Freddie came upstairs, wiping his cheeks vigorously of any wetness that may have fallen there. He lay his head against me, and I wrapped an arm around him.

"When will Papa return?" he queried in a tremulous voice.

"Soon, love. Soon."

"And if he does not?"

"Then we shall sail out to meet him, wherever he may be," I replied as I gave him a kiss on the top of his warm head and placed a hand on my swollen belly. His little face, eyes swollen and red, looked up at me.

"I shall be old enough soon to sail with Father. All the time! Not just going to and from ports, but into battles. I shan't be scared, Mama. I told him he could take me now, for I'll wager that I would be the quickest one in the shrouds!"

"Indeed?" My own eyes were stinging at the thought of that day in the future when I might be sending both of them off to sea.

"Yes, and Papa says that I'll first learn to make oakum from ropes and be a powder monkey below decks. Powder monkey sounds like jolly fun. He says now I have to go and visit Aunt Sophia and Admiral Croft to make sure they have everything shipshape at Kellynch Hall. Will you miss me?"

"Of course, every second. But since Mama cannot play and run with you as I would like, perhaps that would be for the best."

We gave each other another tight squeeze in the way of a formal agreement. My mind wandered over the sad irony that my son would soon be wandering the halls of Kellynch Hall, my ancestral home, as a guest. Had my father been a wiser man, he would be visiting as grandson of the lord in residence.

"Tell my little brother," Freddie continued, placing his small hand on my belly.

"Or sister."

"Yes, or sister, to hurry, as I shall show them the quickest way to scale the birch tree down by the pond. That way they can train for the rigging of a ship with me."

"Of course. I am fully confident that you will be an admirable big brother."

He beamed up at me with that Wentworth grin of his. "I shall make you and Papa very proud."

The next day, Admiral and Mrs Croft came to collect little Freddie. After some tears and hugs, they departed on their way back to Kellynch Hall. I was grateful to have the support of Frederick's sister and her husband, the admiral. My own family were too involved with their own concerns to think it necessary to aid me in times when Frederick was at sea. When not in Bath, Father and Elizabeth were frequently invited to the estate of our cousins, the Dowager Viscountess Dalrymple and the Honourable Miss Carteret. Their presence was deemed absolutely vital to aid the Dalrymples in their constant effort to stave off the plague of boredom and complacency. I could only imagine the long, dreary evenings of cards in enormous, cold halls that had little variety in conversation or company. That would have been my fate as well had I not married Frederick.

My youngest sister, Mary Musgrove, lived nearby with her husband and children. But Mary tended towards a self-absorption that sprang from a propensity for imagining herself ill with little cause and no true symptoms. Some of her boys were away at school, and her youngest were girls. Mary, at least, heeded the call of family obligation enough to visit occasionally and send many letters, although her letters were mostly stuffed with complaints of her own struggles. Her husband, Charles Musgrove, was as attentive as any brother-in-law could be. He frequently sent over game he had hunted. Although I loved my family, I had been more fortunate in finding people who cared for me through marriage and friendship than through birth.

I sat at my window seat in our bedroom, watching the shadows of the early spring clouds on the hill across the valley. It was the burden of a naval officer's wife to always have one eye on the road in case a message should be speeding to her on the back of a horse. It could be a summons for her to join him in some faraway port, an announcement of a promotion, or bad news.

I shook my head to dismiss that last thought. The packet of letters sat next to me on the side table, like an unopened Christmas present. I had tried to keep my mind busy as long as possible to delay the enormous satisfaction of delving into that unposted correspondence. Reading the bundle of letters from Frederick's first year at sea as a captain of the HMS *Asp* had brought us even closer together as man and wife. The trials he faced in the world around him and those he had faced within his own heart were laid bare to me. Things were written that would be very difficult for a man of Frederick's temperament to say aloud, even to his wife. It struck me that his decision to be so vulnerable with his writings was as brave of him as his mightiest choices in battles on the water.

My hand snuck to the pile of letters and took the top one to open. The front of the unopened letter had the familiar writing spilled across it in Frederick's firm, slightly unpolished hand.

Miss Anne Elliot
Kellynch Hall
Somersetshire

My hand ran over the address; I found it touching that he had still addressed and sealed every single one. Frederick himself had not read them since he wrote and closed them years ago. With a start, I realised that if anything had happened to him in battle, if he had not survived, the letters would have been posted to me when they were discovered. If he had died, I would have held these letters in my hands and discovered his unwavering affection for me when it was too late. If that had happened...

Grim thoughts seized my heart. But no matter what the future held for us from this point on, we had had several years of inexpressible happiness to comfort either of us in our grief. With some effort, I breathed deeply and cracked the seal on the first letter. The date was 1808.

Dearest Anne,

Should anyone ever wish to discover what vice that Captain Frederick Wentworth hides from the world, it would be that I cannot defeat the desire to put pen to paper and pour my soul out to you. I sometimes wish I were guilty of excessive drink or losing money at the card table instead. A more manly vice would be one I need not hide from the world. But mine is the rather questionable need to write letters to my former betrothed who has no idea of the existence of said letters. Few were even aware of our pledge to each other. My brother suspected, perhaps. My sister is unaware of your existence. I wish to God you could have known my sister, Sophia. Mrs Sophia Croft, newly married to Captain Croft. I am happy for her, although I am still becoming accustomed to addressing her as such.

I do sometimes wonder, if Sophia had been present during our courtship and brief engagement, if she could have influenced you not to end things as you did. I am sure you would have respected her keen mind and warm heart. Your friend Lady Russell may have had a lesser influence on you if you had heard opinions supporting the continuation of our engagement in the face of disapproval. But speculation is a wager that never pays very well. I must learn to content myself with the idea that you may be happy with another man. I must. Even though the mere idea makes my heart sink and my blood boil.

I had to leave off writing for a few days. The image of you in the warm embrace of another man left me in such a state that I—

I have been given my orders and am to leave the house of my sister and brother-in-law for my new assignment, the HMS *Laconia.* The poor, dear *Asp* was broken up. She treated me with undying affection, even to the last, getting us safe to Plymouth harbour before that four-day storm hit that surely would have sunk us if we had been in the open waters. I am greatly relieved that the Admiralty has seen fit to respect my wishes to have as much of the crew of the *Asp* as I am able to muster. Indeed, I had the honour of receiving a petition of almost all the crew from the *Asp* to tell the Admiralty that they wished to be posted with me again on my next ship. Not every captain can claim such a show of loyalty from their men. It was most touching.

Benwick has received a promotion and is to be my first lieutenant. Your acquaintance, young William Rollins from Somersetshire, is to continue on as a quartermaster, and of course, Owen, my man, to cook for me and look after making me presentable to the world.

I must be allowed to indulge my fancy for a few lines, Anne. Had you been my wife, it would be you, and not Owen, making repairs to all my clothes and gathering together all the delicacies of pickles, wines, sugar, salt, and coffee for me during my time at sea. I am quite certain you would have made for a more pleasing sight to my eyes when my jacket undergoes minor repairs than Owen, good man that he is. And, if I were being assigned to a port, you yourself would be packing up to make a home in some foreign land. Oh, the questions that would have assaulted my ears from your lovely lips! I can hear them in my mind. I think, if you had been given the chance, you would have made a hale and hearty voyager.

I must close this missive. I forbid myself from writing to you for at least several weeks. By that time, I

am sure that I will be prepared to relate the many
grand adventures that Steely Went will have braved.

Yours, Forever and Entirely,

Captain Frederick Wentworth

HMS Laconia (Soon to be)

I closed the letter and pressed it to my chest. I remembered
the instances, late at night, when my sleep had been plagued
by the idea of Frederick in the arms of another woman. It
had been terrible. But beyond the mere physical, the notion
that he had found solace and companionship equal to or
greater than that which we had shared, that was the true
thorn in my side during those eight years of separation.

Never before had the thought occurred to me, that just
now pounced upon my mind, that I may have to read of
Frederick's encounters with other women in these letters. I
remembered his polite flirtation with Catherine LaCroix in
the West Indies just after the termination of our engagement.
But the pain of our rupture was still fresh and raw for him.
He had little difficulty in dismissing the ambitious eye of that
young woman. But now, I was reading of his second year
after our separation. I had my heart steeled to the possibility
of reading of danger, adventure, and injuries. But of feelings
of affection for another?

I briefly recalled Frederick's understandable attraction to
Louisa Musgrove, before she married Captain Benwick. At
that time, we were unaware of each other's still unchanged
feelings of deep regard after the separation of eight long
years. I remembered the toll that took on me, watching their
flirtation bloom. Was I prepared to read of more?

My husband and I rarely revisited that terrible time of

heartache. Choosing instead to focus on the present to make up for lost years, we had not shared with each other everything we went through. But with these letters, my eyes had been opened to what Frederick faced, in the world around him and on the battlefield of his heart.

CHAPTER ELEVEN

In deference to Frederick's effort to moderate writing his letters to me, I made the same effort in reading them. After the first seal of the second stack had been broken, I vowed to limit myself to one letter a day so that I might enjoy them for a longer period of time.

I was in a position to make amends for those years when he ought to have been receiving letters from me as his wife. To that end, I rang the bell for Maude, and she set me up to write to Frederick. By then, if the tides had been cooperative, he may well have been on his way to Tuskar Rock, unravelling the tides and winds to discover the best time to guide the *Bellona* to a port. It could be a dangerous business for a ship coming to the aid of a grounded one. I truly had full confidence in the abilities of my husband, but confidence did little to alleviate worry, especially when I could do so little to occupy my mind and hands.

I wrote to him in a tone warmer than my usual one, telling him he was indeed missed and to hurry his way home when he could. I told of how anxious Freddie was to spend time with Admiral Croft and learn all he could of the proper techniques for making rope into oakum, although I suspected it had been many decades since the admiral had put his hand to such work.

That night, I placed the next letter from Frederick on the table beside our bed so that it would greet me with the rising sun. I fell to sleep with images of swells and waves crashing over the deadly Tuskar Rock and my Frederick on the deck of the HMS *Stoic*, shouting orders and handling it all in his masterful manner.

The next morning, I awoke early and eagerly reached for my next letter. I took a deep breath and opened it.

My Dearest Anne,

Sophia peppered me with questions the morning I left her and Captain Croft's house. I think she suspects that my increasingly foul mood during my visit had a deeper cause than my usual craving for activity. I almost confided in her the tale of our courtship and engagement. But every time I opened my mouth to speak your name, my throat closed up and all thought left my head. It is for me alone to reflect and write. I had not realised that being in the house of a married couple so suited to each other, so full of admiration, humour, and affection would cause me to become morose. Thoughts of what might have been between us, Anne, consumed me every time I witnessed some small act of happiness between them. A look, or touch of the sleeve, gave my heart a leaden feeling.

I am glad to be aboard my newest love, HMS *Laconia*. She is swift, fresh, and ready. It does my heart good to be away from the happy home of my sister. Activity is my path, and I am ready to walk it.

In the close of my last letter, I was being a braggart, building high hopes for adventure. Those hopes have been extinguished as surely as if I had dunked them in the waters of the Baltic Sea. I am to be a courier and guardian of the worst sort of charge.

You will perhaps recall Captain Fowler of the HMS *Seagull?* He, his crew, and the ship were captured by the French. The rumours of the battle paint Captain Fowler in a dim light as a drunken coward who ran at the first sign of trouble. But he is the fourth son of a very influential and wealthy earl. I have strict instructions to limit his access to the rum and wine on the return voyage home. It is a bitter pill indeed for a man like myself to waste valuable time and resources to fetch after this bounder whose only claim to superiority is his birth. It is a bad policy of the navy to forward those in the ranks of the officers who have title and wealth but are ill-suited to the responsibilities. But I have learnt to accept it. Both in my profession and in my heart, I have been dealt harsh blows by not having a more illustrious last name. The only advantage of this rankling affair is that I have had the prisoners we are to exchange, a French captain and a few of his officers, to my cabin to dine. They are to be traded for the invaluable Captain Fowler and his officers. You would be quite proud of my French, Anne. I am able to catch one word out of four and be somewhat assured that I understand it. Benwick, of course, can communicate fluently with them. I suspect I cause the occasional laugh among them at my stumbling words, but it has been a merry change that brightened my mood. I am sorry to say that I will regret trading the French officers for Captain Fowler. I have told Benwick to keep his ears open for any shred of information that may be of use to us that these Frenchmen may drop during times of drinking, but so far they have let nothing slip. They seem to be well-versed in keeping their heads about them, even when the spirits flow freely into their cups. I wish I could say the same of Captain Fowler.

We arrived at the coastal town of La Rochelle, France. Benwick and I rowed ashore with several boats to carry out the exchange of prisoners at the fort there along the coast. We were invited to a brief meeting with Capitaine Toussaint. I was not prepared for the level of civility we were met with. He offered us wine and refreshments. After a while, they brought in Captain Fowler. The mood of Capitaine Toussaint darkened noticeably with the entry of his prize prisoner. A torrent of loud French was unleashed, and I could only catch the words 'wine', 'best', 'excessive', and the name of Captain Fowler repeated often among these complaints. Benwick was obviously uncomfortable at some of the words that were beyond my comprehension.

'Ask Capitaine about the rest of the officers of the *Seagull*, Benwick,' I muttered, pressing down my rising temper at this poor excuse for a British naval officer.

Benwick did. The Capitaine shrugged and gave short answers that seemed to leave Benwick puzzled. Captain Fowler, redder in the face than I remember him being in the West Indies, shuffled his feet and avoided my eye. Finally, in a bellow, Fowler said, 'The dastardly fellows escaped, my crew, my officers, the whole lot of them! Escaped into the night! One of the skinny ship's boys squeezed his way out between the bars and blew up the magazine. They spiked the cannons and ran off without me, Wentworth! They abandoned their captain! The lot of dirty sea dogs are probably back in England by now, curse 'em all to hell! I hope they are tried as pirates, damn them.'

Fowler was positively livid with rage by the time he stopped. Anger and drink made him an alarming shade of burgundy. Toussaint seemed fit to be tied and wanted the pack of us out of his fort. I cannot say that I blamed him. So, although England came out much worse for the deal, we exchanged Fowler for the French officers we had transported. It was a cold, silent boat ride back to the ship.

We are back at Plymouth, and Fowler is finally off my ship and on his way to London to face the tribunal at the Admiralty. I hope they spare no punishment for him. During the trip back, I had surrendered my cabin to Fowler, him being the senior officer of the two of us, and bunked with Benwick. Damned if Fowler did not break the lock on my spirits cabinet and drink a fair bit of my stock. You know me, Anne, I am no drinker, but damn his eyes! The only pleasant moment came when my man Owen, serving me my first dinner alone in my cabin again, muttered to me, 'I'll wager your men would not have left you behind during no prison break, sir. They'd have blown the fort all to bits to get you out, sir.'

'Belay that talk of a superior officer,' I snapped. But I think Owen knows me well enough to see there was little anger and much agreement in my response.

And so ends my first glorious assignment on HMS *Laconia*, dearest Anne. Have a good laugh, as that is the best thing that could come of the whole affair. The only casualty was the lock that protects my wine and some of my best bottles.

Yours, Forever and Entirely,
Captain Frederick Wentworth
HMS Laconia

I shook my head, smiling. Poor Frederick! For a man of his skill, talents, and bravery to be saddled down with the likes of Captain Fowler, it must have been the most ignominious experience. I laughed aloud at the image of him and Benwick cramped together in the first lieutenant's berth on a small frigate while his good wines were being pilfered by the very illustrious fourth son of an earl. He must have been in high dudgeon for several days afterwards. I was relieved that any future letters would have no mention of the former captain, Fowler. What had become of him? He must have faced a court martial at the very least, once the tale of his cowardice and quick surrender was told to the Admiralty. It was wrong of his crew to abandon him so, but I could not say that I blamed them. If drunk, Fowler could have ruined their escape through belligerence and blunder.

Later that day, sitting at the window, I could not resist putting pen to paper again to tell Frederick how much I sympathised with his plight with Fowler. I may not have had as many of the worldly experiences as he, but I was familiar with having to indulge the tempers and whims of volatile family members whose only thought in their heads is their own comfort and pride. It was a unique kind of exhaustion that followed those interactions. Compliments on his conciliatory calm in the face of such a man closed my letter to him.

I glanced out the window and saw a gig flying across the valley. The road was clear and somewhat dried out from our several winter storms, so the vehicle was getting on at a steady pace. It had none of the straining desperation that indicated bad news. After a few moments, I could distinguish two people in the gig. One was a lady, the other a man in uniform.

There was some bustle down below after the gig stopped at our door. I heard the authoritative voice of Maude directing the course of activities. The gig took off again down the road after only a brief interlude, and I heard footsteps on the stairs approaching our bedroom. A young woman followed Maude in and introduced herself as Miss Claire Harville.

"Ah, Captain Harville's eldest daughter?"

"Yes, Captain Wentworth arranged for me to visit with you in the event of his being called up before your-your confinement was complete."

I smiled graciously at the blushing face of this young woman's stumbling embarrassment over the mention of my condition. She was tall, elegant, and her bright blue eyes shone with the excitement of this adventure to a new location. Captain Harville's health kept him confined to Lyme, so I imagined that this little bit of travel was a grand adventure for her.

"I am so glad that you are able to visit with me. I understand you have helped your own mother through her confinements as well."

"Yes, ma'am."

I could plainly see that the exhilaration of the journey and the reticence of her nature combined to make her too hesitant for conversation at the moment. I instructed Maude to see to a room for Claire and to tell Betsy that dinner would need to be a grander affair than the simple meals that I liked.

"Oh no, Mrs Wentworth!" Claire cried. "You need not

make any special arrangements for me. I am very accustomed to plain meals."

"No trouble at all, Claire." I reached out and put my hand on her forearm for her comfort. "Everyone keeps telling me I need to put on some weight. Is that not correct, Maude?"

"Yes ma'am! We all wish you would get more meat on your bones."

"So you see," I continued with a laugh, "my small frame has those who care for me nervous. You will help me to eat a hearty and hale meal every day, I assure you. With the aid of some conversation, perhaps my sparse appetite will increase."

Her nervousness dissolved, and I looked forward to knowing her better. Both of her parents were of an easy and open disposition. There was no lack of conversation with them. It seemed that Claire was of a more thoughtful, quiet turn. For that, I was grateful. In my tired condition, someone who rattled on like a magpie would wear me thin in very short order. Perhaps the effort needed to draw someone of Claire's hesitant nature out would bring some more vigour to me.

CHAPTER TWELVE

T he next morning was brisk and windy. I saw the curtains over the bedroom window flutter ever so slightly as puffs slipped through to ruffle their calm. The day proved to be filled with some novelty. I was grateful, for this unusually quiet confinement of mine had made my mind restless.

Claire was sure to be in later in the morning for reading and needlework. During our dinner the previous night, I had discovered that she, like me, had an affinity for reading. She tended more towards novels of excitement, intrigue, and romance. I tended more towards poetry and philosophy, but regardless, I was always grateful to discover another lover of books.

I had directed her to the location of a few of the newer novels I had in my possession. Her eager eye told me that they would be well appreciated.

I reached my hand over to the next in the series of Frederick's letters. The seal, once broken, was folded back, and my eyes fell greedily on the familiar, scrawling hand of my beloved Frederick.

Dearest Anne,

We have had a jolly time of it on the *Laconia* in the East Indies. We have been instructed to take as many privateers and French merchant ships as we can while also being ready to escort British ships of commerce safely through these waters. Already, we have added to our prize money by the taking of a French frigate.

Benwick has proved himself to be an invaluable asset on more than one occasion, and I have full confidence that should I ever be unable to fulfil my duties as captain, he would step in most admirably. My only complaint with him is that he needs more iron in his style of managing the men. But that assuredness in himself will come in time and practice. He is still but young.

It is hardly a vigorous complaint of Benwick, as the men seem to respect him just as well as myself. Neither of us believe in corporal punishment as being the only path to discipline among the men. The cat-o'-nine-tails is used but rarely on my ships and only in cases of extreme crimes. Some captains take their use of punishments to such an extreme that it borders on acts of evil, but I have seen the looks of resentment and fear those captains get from their men when they believe themselves to be unobserved. I cannot believe men who live in constant fear with hate in their hearts will be willing to give you their all in the heat of battle. I am grateful Benwick and I seem to be in agreement on this point.

A dark cloud hangs over us, Anne. By some miracle

of God, or perhaps I should say a miracle of his father's deep pockets, Captain Fowler has been assigned to accompany me in his ragged frigate, HMS *Mandy*, that has seen more years go by than I care to know. How the Admiralty saw fit to place him in a position of command again, I know not. I can only imagine that they do not want to deal with his folly on land, and his father must feel exactly the same way. The farther away he is, the better. That is the only explanation that makes any sense to me.

What was but a mildly amusing propensity of Captain Fowler's to indulgence in too much wine in the West Indies has burst into a dangerous, daily habit of intoxication that starts in the morning hours and does not cease until his need to lie in a state of insensibility in his cabin overcomes him. I am determined that his bobbing frigate and waves of inebriation will not hinder me in any way in the completion of my sworn duties.

The best thing I can observe of the situation is that the first lieutenant on the *Mandy*, a man named Harville, seems to be a sharp man of action, ready to step in to fill the shoes of his oafish captain when the need arises. He is not the intellectual that First Lieutenant Benwick is, but more of a man of worldly sense and bold action. It is the only blessing of this rummy development. My mood has been gloomy, the millstone of Fowler hanging heavy around my neck, and even Owen steers clear of me when he can. I hope Captain Fowler's incompetence does not cost us men or ships. We have been ordered to accompany five large Indiaman ships back to India from China. Let us hope it is accomplished with few events of note.

Anne, I wish you were here with your way with

words. You have the uncanny ability to know how to speak with others that will create the deepest impression on their mind and heart. I can see you murmuring gently to Fowler, appealing to his sense of duty to better himself in his lack of moderation in drink. How you would go about it, I have no idea. I am too plain-spoken in my dealings to create any of those subtle impressions at which your turn of mind is so adept.

Let us hope that Fowler has been as fortunate in first lieutenants as I have been with Benwick. Harville may be expected to fulfil much more than what is typical for the second-in-command on a frigate. I wish your gentle hand were here to rest on my arm and ease my anxiety on this point. But, barring that, I do seem to derive some measure of comfort from writing to you. For that small solace, I am grateful, dearest Anne.

Yours, Forever and Entirely,
Captain Frederick Wentworth
HMS Laconia

I shook my head as I folded the letter. To be so burdened by a dangerously incompetent fellow captain must have aggrieved Frederick, especially one in a senior station over him. He would be forced to acquiesce to Fowler's orders, even if they were made in a state of intoxication.

It recalled to me the time before my family had to leave Kellynch for Bath due to the worsening lack of management by my father and Elizabeth. It had been torturous to watch our estate fall further and further under debt when a little foresight, frugality, and restraint could set things right. But I was the second daughter, not nearly as beloved by my father as Elizabeth. My opinion meant next to nothing. Even when my voice was joined with Lady Russell's, we could not change the course set by my father. He had set his sails straight for a rocky shore.

The memory caused me to sigh and stand to my feet. I walked slowly to the window and cracked open the curtain. The wind was bending and shaking the branches in a violent fit. Across the valley, a lone rider caught my eye. He was in no hurry, rather he had a jaunty air, as if daring the wind to do its worst. I watched him slowly wend his way to the house.

Once the rider was at the gate, I saw that he had a brace of rabbits hanging from the saddle. It was little Charles Musgrove, son of my sister Mary and Charles Musgrove. Though I can no longer call him little, being a strapping young man of eighteen. He leapt from his horse and slung the rabbits over his shoulder as he walked up the path. I could hear the door opening to him and the voice of Claire Harville greeting him. The usually loud voice of young Charles sounded more bashful and subdued than usual. Smiling to myself and recalling the beautiful face of Claire, I had little doubt as to the cause. Although they had played together often as children, they had not been in each other's company for many years, if my memory served.

I wished I could whisper to Claire to invite him in for a cup of tea, and for her to feel free to sit with him in the parlour for a few minutes. But I saw from the window that young Charles was stepping slowly back to his horse, reluctance leaving a trail behind him as surely as mud on a newly cleaned floor.

Claire burst from the house and detained him at the gate for a few moments of conversation. The bluster of the wind prevented me from overhearing any of their conversation, but I could tell from the fidgeting and stuttered starts to sentences that they both felt uncomfortable in the presence of the other for the best of causes.

I withdrew from the window and foresaw that our table would soon have a surfeit of game from the Uppercross estate. When would young Charles next be racing here with such gifts? Sooner than necessary, I imagined.

In my mind, I mapped out a future path for them. I was powerless to stop my thoughts from treading this course anytime I saw young people who held each other in affection. It was a dreaded impulse that had plagued my mind ever since my own happiness had been refused.

The Harvilles would likely broach no protest in connecting Claire with the Musgrove family. The Musgroves of Uppercross were an ancient Somersetshire family whose income was still very respectable. Young Charles Musgrove reminded me very much of his father. A bit brash, but practical and kindhearted. Claire seemed quiet, thoughtful, and well-read. Perhaps during her stay with me, she would also gain an appreciation for poetry.

With some chagrin, I realised the only opposition would likely come from my own family. If any were to protest a match between Charles and Claire, it would likely come most vehemently from Mary, Elizabeth, and my father. Young Charles Musgrove, grandson of Sir Walter Elliot and heir to Uppercross, likely had pressure from his mother's side of the family regarding who was and was not grand enough a match for him. But fortunately, he had the more sensible and compassionate nature of his father to support him if any such situation should arise. Blood rose to my cheeks. I vowed that if an attachment ever developed between Claire and young Charles that turned to a much deeper regard, they would at least find in me a sympathetic friend who would not throw obstacles in their path.

CHAPTER THIRTEEN

In the morning, I reached for my next letter. Taking time to reflect on each letter made my days go more quickly than if I had been re-reading our collection of books. The next time Mrs Croft ventured to London, I would beg her to return with a new selection of books to help ease the boredom of my confinement and, God willing, the time I might need to recuperate after being brought safely from a healthy child.

Dearest Anne,

I hope I will never be accused of being a trumpeter of my own accomplishments, and I do state my own successes without too much embellishment. But you know that more than anything, I do enjoy a good ruse. And of the following, I am exceedingly proud.

We were accompanying a convoy of five large Indiaman ships from China to India. The *Mandy* and *Laconia* are smaller ships, but we are faster and better trained than the large shipping vessels for all their superior firepower. Both Benwick and I were on deck frequently to scan the waters for any sign of French ships. It was a hazy morning when our eyes spotted the French fleet in the distance. A large ship of the line and four frigates. They must have spotted us and were setting sail in our direction. We would be significantly outgunned by them. Due to the heavy weight of the shipping vessels, our convoy could also be easily outrun. I realised it was Capitaine Durand and his fleet that were here solely to harry and capture British merchant ships.

'Let us hope that Captain Fowler has seen them and will give us orders accordingly,' I muttered to Benwick, wishing rather than believing that Fowler was level-headed and not in his cups.

Benwick fiddled with the spyglass for a moment and cleared his throat.

'Spit it out, man!' I snapped.

'Perhaps, sir, I should look towards the HMS *Mandy* and ascertain whether their captain is on deck yet.'

I knew what it meant for the rest of the crew to see us ogling the *Mandy* like that. It would tell them we had no confidence in Captain Fowler. Which was the truth. I glanced at the five Indiaman ships behind us, loaded to the brim with cargo, millions of pounds worth. The loss of them would be a blow to England.

'May Fowler drown in his cups one day and relieve us all of his burdensome self! Yes! See what you can observe on the deck of the *Mandy*!'

After a moment, Benwick lowered the spyglass and muttered to me, 'I see First Lieutenant Harville, observing us, through a spyglass. Captain Fowler is nowhere to be seen on deck, sir.'

Anne, you will be ashamed to know that I whispered out such a torrent of invectives that the fish in the water must have blushed. Benwick wisely pretended to be inspecting the rigging overhead, and once I relieved my heart of that burden, I gave him orders to run flags up to message our fleet to form a line of battle.

'This haze may make Durand unable to see that we are but two frigates. These merchant ships will look much like ships of the line from this distance. He will think twice before sailing up to us to open fire if he thinks we are five warships and two frigates. It will be the ruse of a lifetime, eh Benwick?'

'Yes, sir.'

We ran up the flags, the Indiaman merchant ships lined up as if they were the finest ships of war ever to serve in His Majesty's Navy. Harville, on the *Mandy*, completed the line on the other side. Our port sides were to the approaching ships. I watched Harville through the spyglass, managing it very well. I turned my eye back to the French, who were just now coming within shooting distance.

'Pipe to quarters!'

The men rolled up the cannons and opened the portside gunports. I gave the order for a volley from all of our ships, to show the French what sort of bees' nest they were rustling at. Bless my soul, Anne, my ruse worked! The French slowed, sails raised and lowered, and they turned to reverse course. Captain Durand mistakenly thought he was engaged with a large British fleet, not a few frigates and merchantmen. Benwick actually smiled at me, even his enjoyment of the ruse could not be disguised.

A thought came to me that we might rid ourselves

of this fleet if I could maintain the ruse. If Durand ever realised his mistake, he could order his fleet to turn around and hunt us down. We would be back in the original jeopardy we had just eluded. Till we were safely through the Straits of Malacca, we were still in danger from Durand. It is a dangerous passage that would be more dangerous if Durand discovered his mistake and came at us full force, compelling us to make unwise decisions in dangerous waters.

'Raise the flags to give chase, Benwick.'

'Sir?'

'You heard me! We are going to give chase! Move it, man!'

'Yes, sir.'

So there we were, two frigates and five Indiamen giving chase for several hours to a French ship of the line and her frigates. It was the most fun that I have had in some time, Anne. I could see the crews of the merchant ships whooping it up and laughing, unaccustomed as they were to such sport. It must have been a pleasant change for them from always being the ones being hunted. After several hours of this, I felt confident that we would make it through the Straits of Malacca without the worry of that French fleet catching us unawares. I gave the order to break off the chase. It was one of the most pleasant entries I have ever made in the ship's log, and I wonder at the expression of the Admiralty when they read of it. I made certain to pointedly make a note of the excellent conduct of First Lieutenant Harville without actually accusing Captain Fowler of a dereliction of his duties. Hopefully, those who read of it will see what I have said in my silence.

As you see, my propensity towards occasionally

dissembling is not an entirely dark mark on my character. I know it always intrigued you when we were forced by propriety to leave the isolation of our contented companionship and into an evening of cards. Although I am generally not a passionate card player, I did receive real pleasure at seeing how far a good ruse could get me. Your twinkling eye across the table from me, trying to discern the true motives of the plays I made, that was the reward for me. Although I can hear you disagree with me on this point and become mired in the fine distinction between a ruse and a lie, I find that those hours spent at the card table and not in conversation with you were not a total waste. I wish we could have one of our lively discussions so I could have the opportunity to turn your mind to my way of thinking. Our happy quarrels full of laughter are one of the things I miss most, dear Anne.

Your, Forever and Entirely,
Captain Frederick Wentworth
HMS Laconia

I clearly remembered those nights, wrapped in a card game from which neither of us derived true pleasure, wondering what Frederick was about when he played cards that were not to his benefit. His clever mind saw many possibilities and recorded previous cards played with ease. He would sigh, shake his head, furrow his brows in a show of false anxiety to encourage the belief among the others that the hand he was dealt was wretched. I had to exert a great effort to not laugh aloud at his display. In several instances, I had to lower my head to disguise my mirth. But Frederick's gamble worked highly in his favour. Later, I would take him to task for his theatrics and point out to him that leading people into a false belief that he held disadvantageous cards was a form of lying.

"No, Miss Anne," he had said. "Here we must agree to disagree. A ruse is a form of acting that carries no inherent evil unless it is used for dark purposes. Acting is a skill that carries no inherent evil, but very well may be transformative for good. Think of all the good that can come from theatrics! And until you can tell me that the words of the most genius poets and playwrights have not helped fan deep love, enduring passion, a most sincere regard for one who has captured my heart..."

I recalled that Frederick broke off his train of thought and turned from me with a blush. But perhaps we had just been standing too close to the warm fire that evening. We had certainly been standing too close to each other. I knew that my cheeks had glowed as he terminated his sentence mid-thought and I took a step back. I believe he had asked for my hand in marriage a very few days later. Remembrances of our conversations had helped me through those bleak eight years that we were separated.

CHAPTER FOURTEEN

Through the open window, I could smell the spring flowers and hear the sounds of an approaching carriage. I moved carefully to the window and was greeted by the familiar form of Lady Russell's horses. A good conversation with my friend was always a welcome interlude. I marvelled at the many comings and goings along our quiet road in the valley of late. It had helped me enormously to keep my mind from lingering too long on a difficult confinement or Frederick's dangerous mission.

Lady Russell was shown to my room after I was dressed and sat opposite me as I had some breakfast. I knew well that our long-standing friendship could survive the impropriety of her attending me in my bedchamber as I ate.

"Anne, dear, it does my heart good to see your appetite still whetted so close to your delivery," she said after giving me a kiss on the cheek and sitting across from me. "You are not nearly so round as you became with Freddie, and that was a mild delivery, as I recall."

"I credit the ease of that confinement to the rolling of the ship beneath my feet early on. It may be that the sea has a medicinal effect that is unknown to physicians."

"Perhaps. This business of childbirth is such a treacherous affair that I can hardly understand why—"

Her tongue paused after this last statement, as she seemed to wisely check the flow of words in order not to denigrate my present state. Lady Russell had never had children and possessed a dim view of the entire institution. She blamed the birth of my youngest sister, Mary, for the steady decline in the health of her best friend, my mother, Lady Elliot. Perhaps she was correct on some points, and I suspect that was one of the reasons she never sought a remarriage after the death of her husband. To her, childbirth was an experience to be avoided at all costs by women of means.

To divert the subject, Lady Russell lifted a bundle of books tied with string to the tabletop.

"Oh, thank you so much. My library has been quite worn over with my readings. And with Frederick gone off, I am unable to send him to London to procure me new additions. A novel, too!"

"Yes, by Mary Shelley, author of *Frankenstein*. This one is entitled *Valperga*."

"I remember reading *Frankenstein* a few years after my marriage. I was sailing with Frederick in the north. I stayed awake all night and could hardly sleep the next, I was that frightened! You know I rarely am so carried away by a novel, but that one truly caused me some sleepless nights. It was my circumstances, perhaps, that increased my terrors. To be sailing in cold waters while reading of the monster disappearing into the ice flows of the Arctic Circle was a chilling trial for my nerves."

"This is more of a romance, but with some powerful points put forward in the ring of politics. I think you will enjoy it."

"A romance? I have a guest, young Claire Harville, who will enjoy it. Every girl of seventeen will take more delight in a romance. She seems to admire the romantic novels very much, and my collection of them is rather thin."

"Hmm. I suspect that the intricacies of the political debate within the novel will be above her. Harville? Claire Harville, you say? Is not that the family who cared for Louisa Musgrove after she had that foolish tumble from the steps in Lyme?"

"Yes, after Louisa's terrible fall, the Harvilles cared for her and nursed her back to health. Indeed, it is likely that the very careful tending that she received from them is the reason she is alive today. Louisa married Captain Benwick, a good friend of Frederick's. I believe it was at the Harvilles' that Louisa and Benwick first developed an attachment. Over poetry, most likely. Benwick is very well-read, and Louisa had time during her recuperation to develop a love of poetry."

"A sea captain who knows poetry? How unusual. I have found that—" Lady Russell paused, clearly reflecting on her words in the house of a most beloved captain. "It could be said that the tastes of most men of the navy are not quite that refined, although there are exceptions, I am sure."

Inwardly, I mourned the loss of our once completely frank discussions. Our friendship remained strong, but it would likely never be what it was before I refused to marry my cousin and ensure my place as the next Lady Elliot. To imagine that I would overthrow the intentions of so many and relinquish the right to become Lady Elliot of Kellynch Hall would forever be a mystery to Lady Russell, as would be my eagerness to become wife to a navy captain. I smiled privately at her misspoken words and pretended to be busy arranging my breakfast things on my tray.

"Are the Harvilles a family of means?" Lady Russell resumed.

"Captain Harville, although an excellent officer whom I have had occasion to see in action personally, never had as much luck as Frederick at capturing prize ships during the war. He is fairly well set up, but not to the extent of Frederick or Benwick, I believe."

"Hmm."

I could see behind her eyes that the machinations for calculating a match that was good, but not too far above Claire's station, were already lurching forward in Lady Russell's mind. I thought it best not to introduce the topic of Claire and young Charles Musgrove's meeting the day before. As self-appointed guardian of all the affairs of the Elliot family, she would hardly look on a fond attachment between the two with any approbation.

I supposed that I must brace myself for future conflicts of this nature, as the Musgrove children were just entering into that interesting age of seeking out a partner in life. The elders of their families would no doubt have many pointed opinions on any prospective matches. The marriage of Mary and Charles Musgrove had garnered her sincere endorsement. My marriage to Wentworth had eventually had her begrudging approval once she saw my happiness and his truly deep admiration for me. Elizabeth remained single, a state that I thought she was well suited for. Young Charles was the grandson of Sir Walter Elliot. An Elliot marrying the daughter of an injured captain of limited means would be no feather in Lady Russell's cap. I kept my suspicions of a growing attachment between Claire and young Charles to myself, something that I was very well practised at.

After a pleasant morning discussing books and the latest news of the world and our acquaintances, Claire joined us.

Lady Russell appeared well impressed by Claire's gracious, shy manners and becoming face. Claire was still too uncertain in her social abilities to feel at ease with one whose presence was as imposing as that of Lady Russell. Her short answers to Lady Russell's many questions must have frustrated my old friend.

Both ladies soon noticed that I was becoming weary, and as they took their leave, I overheard Lady Russell promise a nice stack of passionate novels for Claire when she next visited.

Maude entered and cleared the breakfast things.

"I'm glad the two ladies are leaving you to yourself for a bit, Mrs Wentworth. I was quite ready to grab my broom and shoo them off. You'll be needing a rest soon."

"Quite right. It is well that Claire seems to be the sort of girl who needs little encouragement to find her own amusement. Having her here is pleasant, but I do tire easily these days."

"Bless my soul!" Maude exclaimed as she peered out of my window.

"What is it, Maude?" I asked, secretly fearful that the bleak chunk of rock off the coast of Ireland had managed to procure another victim by wrecking the HMS *Stoic*. But my fears were unfounded. Maude turned to me with a very knowing grin.

"If it is not young Mr Charles Musgrove, with a brace of pheasants slung across his saddle. Just how much does he think a house full o' ladies can manage to eat?"

I smiled as I sat on the bed with care. It was very well that Lady Russell was not here to observe his arrival. I was grateful that I would not hear my sister Mary's screeching enquiries to young Charles as to the meaning of another trip so soon to visit me. It would elicit either jealousy or suspicion, two emotions that Mary flew to quickly. And when it came to her precious first son, her volatile temper was even more susceptible.

"Once you, Betsy, and Jim have eaten your fill, you can send any extra game we may have home with the housemaid or to the cottages down the way."

"Yes, ma'am."

"Also, Maude, I suspect you should be—" I was about to say on guard and thought better of it. "—aware that it is entirely likely that my sister Mary will be curious about all this sudden attention that young Charles is showing his favourite aunt. His justification of fond memories of me nursing him closely through his broken collarbone will not convince her for very long that I am the principal cause of so many trips here."

"She is a keen one, your sister. I hope she'll not henpeck Miss Harville to pieces when she does visit."

"That will be all, Maude. Thank you," I said, aware that her conversation was bordering on rudeness to the daughter of Sir Walter of Kellynch. But the truth of her words struck me as a very fair assessment of the situation. I sighed as I settled back with one hand on my enormous belly. Was it a common occurrence for relations to be a cause of so much concern? Frederick and his sister were all affability when they met, aside from good-humoured teasing that came from a long history of love and support. Although their childhoods had been more difficult in terms of worldly concerns, the bond between them was enviable.

A kick woke me just as I dozed, and I felt a giant shifting within.

"Not long now, eh, little one?" I murmured as I hoped rather than expected that Frederick would be there when the time came.

The next morning, even through the curtains, I could see the shadow of a few bursting pods of tight little leaves on the branches outside my window. The Vile Rooster, seemingly excited by this development, bellowed the news long and loud for the entire world to hear. I pushed myself up, heaving hard as I frequently saw the men aboard ships do with the damp, hefty sails. Resting for a moment from so much activity, I grabbed the next letter from the bedside table.

I had neglected to place it there myself and thought that Maude must have done it for me. What must she think of all these sealed and worn letters that I opened slowly?

I snapped the brittle seal and read.

Dearest Anne,

Although the cloud of Fowler (I can no longer bring myself to write the rank of captain before his name; it profanes the title too greatly for my conscience to bear it in this private letter) still hangs over us, our company has been brightened by the addition of Captain Austen of the HMS *St Albans*. We are to be joined by him for our current assignment of safely escorting a convoy of Indiaman ships. It lifts my spirits considerably to have the company of such a capable fellow captain. Owen told me that the East India Company was so grateful to him for the safe escort of a recent convoy of considerable value that he was given over 400 pounds. Perhaps we shall still have his company for some time to come.

When Captain Austen joined us, he brought the very welcome addition of a mailbag. I had letters from both my sister and brother to enjoy from it. But from that very same bag came a scare that was far worse than anything that might plague me in battle. Rollins received a letter from home. I have made it a regular habit to enquire politely after the Elliot family as well as his own. To my shock, he informed me of the marriage of one of the younger Elliot daughters. Anne, for a moment, I swear that Charybdis opened her maw beneath me and swallowed me from this world. For a few seconds, the sky blackened and I was beyond all thought.

'Miss Anne Elliot is married, then?' I followed up with the best imitation of nonchalance that my stopped heart could muster.

'No, sir. Miss Mary is lately married. The youngest daughter of Sir Walter Elliot of Kellynch Hall. The two eldest are still at home, I believe.'

'Ah, I see.'

He spoke further as to with whom and when this happy event occurred, but I could not attend to a single word of it for the rush of blood that sounded in my ear like a drum beating.

'Thank you, Mr Rollins,' I think I said. 'It is good of you to inform me as to the goings-on of a county that I spent several pleasant months in.'

I managed to make it back to my cabin and collapse in a heap at my desk. When Owen came in with my dinner, I sent it away and asked for some strong spirits instead. I am sure he thought me addled and asked if I needed the doctor.

'No, damn it, just a stiff drink and leave me be for the rest of the evening.'

I went to my bunk and fell into a listlessness that stayed with me for the rest of the evening. What if it had been the announcement of your own marriage, Anne? I must somehow acclimate my mind to the notion that you will indeed take another as your husband one day. I must. I shall. In the future, a letter young Rollins receives may very well contain the news of some lucky man succeeding in winning your heart and mind. I must inure my heart to the idea so well that I may meet you in the street one day and nod and be civil. We shall even exchange inane pleasantries that you and I always found such a chore. These feelings of mine must be diluted to such an extent that you may view me as cool and aloof and wonder that we had ever had any sort of understanding between us.

Your Obedient Servant,

Captain Frederick Wentworth

HMS Laconia

I blinked back a few tears, surprised by the surge of sorrow from that small but potent omission in the closing of his letter. My mind lectured my heart in a stern voice of the good sense he was displaying in his reasoning. But my heart, like a child perceiving an injustice where there had been none, cried out its sorrows.

I, too, had attempted many times to convince myself that my reaction to any news of Frederick marrying another would cause me no pain. It was only logical that a man of his hale and hearty good looks, fortune, and standing would wed and settle with another. A rejection from me did not mean that he would ever be greeted with another upon a proposal of marriage to an entirely different woman.

I shook my head at our mutual foolishness. When we did

finally meet again, eight years after our first engagement ended, neither of us had accomplished that simple, rational task of erasing the other from our hearts. It was a failure for which both of us were eternally grateful.

The rest of the day was quiet, with no visitors pounding down the road to disturb the tranquillity of the warmth filled with birdsong. Poor Claire often got up from her needlework to gaze out of the window. For two days in a row, young Charles had ridden here. It was natural that she would anticipate him for a third day.

I smiled as I bent over my needlework. "Young Charles has certainly been generous in his gifts to this house."

"Yes!" Claire declared with a burst of warmth. "And it has been truly the most delicious game that I have ever tasted!"

I doubted that Claire had had much, if any, fresh game in her life, having grown up on the coast in a family with no property. But the heart is always so enthusiastic in dwelling on the merits of one who has captured its affections.

Later in the afternoon, when the sun was too far along to allow time for a visitor from Uppercross, Claire became low in spirits and claimed that a headache was beginning to plague her. It was then that I knew it was more than a passing fancy on her part. I hoped young Charles felt the same.

CHAPTER FIFTEEN

D awn met me with a blush of reddish clouds. I was
awake much earlier than usual and felt the restlessness that the commencement of spring always gave
rise to in my bones. I reached for my next letter from
Frederick.

Dear Anne,

My spirits continue to be jolly with the addition of
Captain Austen to our convoy guardian duties. It has
been a relatively calm few weeks of little to report. No
prize ships have been taken by us, but one must always
believe that the unseen beyond the horizon holds glory
and wealth.

Captain Austen is more a card player than the rest
of us. Although I hold some talent at Whist, I often
only participate out of the necessity of being asked. On
a ship, excuses that can be made to beg off are fewer.
But, as when I played with you, I find that the better

the company, the more enjoyable the game. Fowler has been at our dinners less frequently due to 'low spirits' which, I imagine, is his way of saying he is fearful that he is too drunk to make the swaying climb from his boat up the rope ladder dangling off the side of the ship. I regret to say that his attendance is rarely missed.

Frequently, after dinner, cards are played to keep the mind sharp during this relatively peaceful time of few enemy ships to harry us. It has also been useful to learn of techniques to ensure that one's crew is always at their best when it is time for action. Captain Austen has made quite the study of how a crew may do their best through high-quality food. Barrels of lime juice are always on his ships, and he makes a point of obtaining as many items of fresh fruit and vegetables from ports as he puts into. It is his opinion that, although our navy supplies a very good diet to its seamen when compared with other navies of the world, more improvement could be made on this point, as it can be as decisive a factor to winning a battle as any other.

'In fact,' Captain Austen said, 'there was a time when I was engaged in actions with Swedish ships against the Russians. The poor Swedish crew were so afflicted with scurvy that they were unable to man their cannons properly. As you well know, manning a cannon is no job for the feeble. The proper feeding of a crew can mean the difference of a win or loss. The Swedish ships were fortunate our men were in better health and able to swing the battle to our advantage. Had we not been present with the healthier men to haul the cannons back and forth for reloading, the Russians would have overrun the Swedish fleet.'

I also discovered we had both been present at the

Battle of San Domingo. He brought up the lee line of the ships as captain in the HMS *Canopus* while I was still a first lieutenant. It was a treat to carefully talk over the battle and the strategies employed by the excellent command of Vice Admiral Duckworth. We did commiserate over the fact that neither of us had been present for the Battle of Trafalgar due to other assignments. To have missed that day, both glorious in battle and tragic in the death of Vice Admiral Nelson, will always be a regret of mine.

After many meals tolerating the barely coherent ramblings of Fowler, intelligent conversation that informs and educates has been like a breath of fresh air. Whatever good soul in the Admiralty who bestowed on me such an amiable fellow captain as is Captain Austen has my eternal gratitude.

That was a difference between us, Anne. I never lacked for invigorating discussions with my family while growing up. Both my brother and sister are two of the brightest people I have known. We may have experienced hardships in the early loss of our parents and lack of wealth or family name, but lively evenings by the fire discussing what we had read that day were a balm that made the other miseries lessen their hold.

It seemed to me, aside from your acquaintance with Lady Russell, you were in a veritable desert of intelligent dialogue. I refrain from saying a large number of things against Lady Russell and the evil she wrought between us, but one thing I cannot accuse her of is a lack of a thinking mind. I wish to God she had turned that mind of hers to convincing Sir Walter of the very great advantage of having a captain married to his middle daughter. Perhaps, if she had worked *for* us instead of against us, our lives may have turned out very differently. I can only guess that it was she who had the most profound influence in your decision to break off from our engagement. I suspect that had Lady Russell been in support of our marriage, you may well have risked the disfavour of your father and married me.

You could be here at my side on these voyages, Anne, and see the wonders of the world for yourself instead of only through the words on a page. To hear your observations upon seeing a red moon of frighteningly large size rising on the horizon. Your gasp of amazement as the sea around us glows the brightest of colours in the dark of a warm, calm night from the bow of our ship passing by, what we call the burning of the sea. There are wonders out here that any amount of reading and imagination cannot fully prepare you for.

All I can wish is that you have found some true measure of happiness back in England and that I will endeavour to persevere in my campaign to erase all knowledge of you from my heart. Progress is slow, but already I feel less despondent. Instead of confronting each day in a wash of sorrow, it is a splash of melancholy. If I could just encounter a woman whose countenance is as intriguing, her mind as cultivated, her humour as warm as yours, her heart as loving, maybe there is a chance I can be happy again. Does such a woman exist?

Your faithful servant,
Captain Frederick Wentworth
HMS Laconia

I rested the letter on my lap. My mind traced its way through the many wonders I had been witness to during my voyages with Frederick. He was correct in his judgment that words alone could not do justice to the marvels there were to witness on a ship at sea. As much as I believed in the enormous power of a phrase well turned, the burning of the sea on a balmy, still night was a wonder that left me speechless. Witnessing St Elmo's fire burnishing into the night sky from the top of the masts, the hissing of it calling to us, just before a strong thunderstorm overtook us was perhaps the most wondrous thing I had witnessed during my time on board a ship. I looked out at the calm English countryside and counted myself fortunate to have had so many adventures and lived to tell the tale. It made the quiet moments at home that much sweeter.

I had had no better luck in those eight years in finding one whom I could place above Frederick Wentworth in my heart. Did there exist such a man? I smiled to myself and placed a hand on my stomach. I thought not. Not for me, anyway.

I had received two other proposals of marriage in the time between Frederick's proposals. The first had been from Charles Musgrove, heir to Uppercross. Charles, being now married to my younger sister Mary, seemed happy in his life, although my sister did try his nerves with her restless mind that never seemed settled or content. If I had accepted, Charles and I could have had a very successful marriage. If I had not first met Frederick, perhaps I would have accepted him, and I would have been called Anne Musgrove of Uppercross instead. Charles was not unintelligent, possessing a kind heart and an open, friendly nature. There was a good chance that my reading may have inspired him to improve his mind as well.

The second proposal had been a very different sort of

affair all together. William Elliot, next in line to be the lord of Kellynch Hall when my father died, had proposed to me just days before Frederick offered his hand to me for the second and last time. William Elliot was a very intelligent, shrewd man. But his heart lacked warmth and his soul was devoid of compassion. It was a hard thing to sacrifice the possibility of being the next Lady Elliot of Kellynch Hall, but there had been no passion for him within my heart that I could mould into a warm, respectful love.

Charles Musgrove could have made my heart happy, but not my mind. William Elliot could have made my mind happy, but my heart would have been cold and, I suspect, occasionally wounded by callousness. I was quite sure the outside world marvelled at the fact that I had passed by two such eligible matches, especially since almost no one knew of my time with Frederick. I sighed long, thinking of him out at sea, trying to wrestle with the exact demons I had been battling with in England.

CHAPTER SIXTEEN

After my breakfast, Claire and I had just settled in for a quiet morning of needlework and conversation when I heard the rumble of a carriage in the distance.

Claire sprang up with a glow in her face.

"Who is coming this way, Claire?"

After a brief description of the carriage, I cried, "It sounds like the carriage of my sister and brother of Uppercross. How delightful. I have not seen them for quite some time, as Mary rarely leaves her home for anywhere other than Bath or London."

I failed to add that I doubted concern for me was the reason for this sudden visit. I knew very well how rapidly Mary could form suspicions. She must have been very curious as to exactly why young Charles had ridden here two days in a row.

Claire fiddled with the edge of the curtain, twining it in her fingers and plucking at a stray thread mercilessly.

"I wonder," I speculated aloud, "whether young Charles

has accompanied his father and mother?"

"Yes! That is to say, perhaps. I mean, he is so busy with hunting, as the weather is fine lately, that he may not have been able to spare the time. So, perhaps, no, he may not be with them. I would imagine there is much to do on the estate at this time of year, although I know little of the ways of farming, growing up by the sea. I imagine there is much he must attend to, do you not, Mrs Wentworth? With all of the fields and animals?"

"I imagine that, yes, the fields and animals take up much of young Charles's time at the moment."

I looked down to hide my smile at her sudden explosion of enthusiasm. I suspected that she had never turned her mind to the intricacies of estate management before.

"Mary will have something to say about the inconvenience of a muddy spring road," I said. "Claire, fetch me my shawl, please. I wish to go down to the parlour and greet them. Otherwise, I am sure Charles will blush terribly at the idea of coming to my bedchamber to pay his respects."

"Oh, Mrs Wentworth! Are you sure that is wise? Maude will be in a bustle about it!"

"Despite what Maude may have everyone believe, I am truly the mistress of this house," I said with a wry smile. "A bit of movement may do me a world of good. This baby is past the time when they should have made their grand entrance. Being on my feet may provide the encouragement needed to move things along. The worst thing for a ship is to stay in port too long. It does more harm to the vessel than good."

"If you say so," Claire responded with wide eyes as she swept the shawl over my shoulders and took my elbow for the slow descent downstairs.

I felt very much like a grand ship being towed along in a harbour too slim to accommodate me by a very small but capable tow boat. We shuffled into the parlour just before Maude, who discovered our foray with a giant huff and a rain of mutterings, opened the door for our guests.

Mary and Charles were ushered into the parlour. Charles came over immediately to take my hand and bow over it with a warm smile.

"Anne! You look very well indeed. A little flushed, perhaps, but very well. I can see that the game young Charles has been bringing has done your blood some good! Nothing raises your energy like some fresh rabbit."

"Charles!" Mary hissed at him, no doubt thinking the discussion of the state of a woman's blood when she was with child improper. With a little bump into his side, she cleared the way to give me a proper look up and down.

"There was so much talk of this confinement being difficult for you that I had to come and see for myself. Of course, it was all hopeless exaggeration, I see. I can tell by the colour of your cheeks that you are very well indeed. I am not sure why you were telling everyone that you were not in the best of spirits. You surprise me, sister. To spread about such gossip when the truth of the matter is entirely different is not like you at all."

"Mary, dear," I smiled up at her. "It was not me telling others of any such diagnoses, I assure you. Wherever you may have come across that information, please inform them that I am doing well and feel just a bit more fatigue than I did with little Freddie."

But my sister had stopped listening to my efforts to stem worrisome gossip long before my last sentence left my mouth. Her eyes were looking over dear Claire as I had frequently seen local farmers evaluate a particularly fine horse in front of an inn while its rider was taking in a pint of refreshment within. I doubted that Claire's gentle beauty had escaped Mary's sharp eye.

Poor Claire, who had probably not anticipated any such scrutiny, flustered about with the back of my chair and cleared her throat in a forced, strangled manner.

"Mary, you remember the Harvilles who nursed Louisa back from that terrible fall at Lyme. This is their eldest daughter, Claire. Frederick arranged for her to keep me company in case he should be called away while my time was near."

Mary tore her gaze from Claire to turn and sit. "I am very pleased to be acquainted with you, Miss Harville," she managed in a cold tone.

"I am very pleased to meet you again, Mrs Musgrove. I have many fond memories of playing at Uppercross when your sister took ill at Lyme. It was such a wonderful time for me, although the cause of it was indeed terrible."

"I do recall those days," replied Mary. "The Great House at Uppercross was positively teeming with little Harvilles. I remember a series of headaches during those months."

"Headaches that repeated visits to Lyme caused to disappear entirely, my dear," Charles put in. "It is wonderful to see you again, Miss Harville! It has been too many years. Indeed, you have bloomed into quite the becoming young woman, if I may say so. If Anne can spare you one afternoon, you must come see us at Uppercross!"

Mary gave a startled look at her husband who had apparently not consulted her. "I am sure Anne cannot possibly spare her, Charles! She is much too valuable here as a companion, or to fetch the doctor should the need arise."

"I would be more than willing to have Claire treated to a visit to Uppercross," I said, smiling. "I am well attended here, as you know."

"Then it is settled," Charles pressed on. "How about the carriage comes for you tomorrow morning, Miss Harville?"

I glanced up at Claire and nodded a little encouragement.

"Of course, yes! I would be delighted. Thank you so much for the invitation."

Mary, tugging furiously at the creases in her gown and straightening her shawl, asked sharply, "So, where has Frederick run off to now? What could possibly be so important to cause him to abandon you at a time like this?"

"He was asked to float a ship off the Tuskar Rock near Ireland. A large ship that the navy wanted handled with care by an experienced, trusted hand. I doubt the state of his wife's condition was a consideration for the Admiralty when the fate of a ship like the HMS *Bellona* is at stake."

"Well, if he would rather be wandering the world than seeing to the health of his family—"

"Mary," Charles cut in, "I am sure Frederick will be back and by her side as soon as he possibly can."

"And how," I ventured, in an effort to steer the subject from one that caused me worry, "have you settled into the Great House? Is your mother comfortably settled into your old cottage to her satisfaction, Charles?"

"Yes, she has overcome some of the melancholy from the loss of Father, but she still has her days when she does not venture forth like she used to."

I leant towards Charles and touched his arm. "It is a testament to how beloved your father was. By many. I am very glad I could count him among my closest and dearest acquaintances."

Charles grinned sheepishly. I saw his eyelids blink rapidly as he dropped his gaze down. I inhaled deeply and turned my full attention to Mary, who was making furtive glances at Claire.

"Was young Charles detained at home today, Mary? He has been so very kind in his remembrance of us while Frederick is gone. I hope he is well."

"Very well, thank you." Mary gave one piercing glance at

Claire, probably hoping to glean some insight into the young woman's feelings for her eldest son. I prayed that I would have the sense to be less obtrusive in my son's matters of the heart when the time came. But who knew? Perhaps I would be just as officious and curious as she. It was hard to say when one's child was still so young. Had Mary any sense in the matter, she would know that one of the surest ways to create an attachment between young hearts was to express one's disfavour of it.

"As you can see, Anne, spring is upon us, and it is the time of the year when the future heir of Uppercross should busy himself by attending to the properties and fields. I am quite certain that, henceforth, he will have very little time to spare for gallivanting around the shrubs, scaring up every little piece of game to be had, and toting them here himself. I was a little cross—"

"A little? Ha!" Charles exclaimed.

"A *little* cross," Mary continued, "when I discovered how very much time he had wasted in bringing you game from our estate. Imagine, a few women…" She paused, looking up at Claire. "A few women and a *girl*, needing so many hares and pheasants. Ridiculous!"

"Come now, Mary! You know in what high regard young Charles holds his aunt Anne who nursed him so faithfully when his collarbone was broken! It shows a very admirable, grateful respect for which the boy ought to be praised, not censured."

Charles ended his rational speech with a knowing glance at Claire. I foresaw many lively discussions between Charles and Mary regarding the suitableness of potential wives for their son. I knew Charles held the Harvilles in the highest regard for their excellent character and their nursing of his sister Louisa several years before.

"All I know," Mary cut in authoritatively, "is that young

Charles has many skills to learn and refine in order to prepare for his future at Uppercross. And I am sure, when the time comes, years from now, he will bring home a proper bride who will do justice to the Elliot and Musgrove names. But that subject should be far from our consideration, he is so young. Indeed, we need not consider it for many years, I imagine."

Fortunately, with her innate sense of timing, Maude bumped the door open and brought in a tray of tea and refreshments. I was glad for the intrusion to bring the topic to a close. Claire, to her credit, cut a very elegant figure with her sweeping, golden curls as she poured out the tea and served everyone with impeccable manners. The only indications to show her true feelings at that moment were a rosy hue to her cheeks and a stiffness in her long neck. I was glad to see this sign of iron in her. To possibly put up with my sister as a future mother-in-law, she would need some strength in her character. Fortunately, she seemed to be one of those quiet, reflective souls who hid their true fortitude until the moment came and they rose to meet it. Mary would be wise to hold her tongue more and create some warmth between them. But, as usually happened when I was separated from Frederick, my observations went unspoken and were for myself alone. I sincerely doubted that Mary would take any of my advice anyway. My family held my thoughts and insights very cheaply indeed.

When plans had been made for Claire to join the Musgroves the following day at Uppercross and their carriage had left, I wearily sat back in my chair and gathered up the energy needed to return to my chambers. Claire and Maude helped me up the stairs from what I sensed would be my last trip downstairs for a while. Once settled into bed for the evening, I dozed off rapidly into a dreamless sleep that lasted through the night.

CHAPTER SEVENTEEN

I awoke the next morning, somewhat refreshed, eager to see Claire off to her visit to Uppercross. But before that could occur, I simply had to read my next letter from Frederick. In the mild light of dawn, I reached and grasped the next, and final, letter placed there by Maude the night before.

Dear Anne,

I hardly know what to write, but Captain Fowler is dead. I cannot help but feel some regret for the way I spoke of him, now that he is beyond endangering both of our crews and our ships.

It was quite an unexpected shock due to the fact that it occurred during a relatively mild battle with no other deaths and very few injuries incurred. If I had a mind that was more bent to seeing the hand of God in the activities of this world, I would swear that it seemed to be divine intervention of some sort. I wish I had your steady blend of faith and poetry to counsel me here right now. I feel utterly wretched saying this of any man, but I know for a fact that we are better off.

Poor Harville is now acting captain of the HMS *Mandy*. The crew of the *Mandy* do not in any way appear to be in the throes of mourning at the change. I wish I had better things to say of Fowler, but a captain so derelict in his duties was a danger to those who served under him and beside him. I am forced to take your broader view of things and wonder whether he suffered in ways that I could not imagine and he only found solace and comfort in his cups.

Here on these pages to you is the only place I may vent my feelings without hesitation. The ship's log that will be the official record sent to the Admiralty can have none of these private observations. I cannot voice them aloud, even to Benwick. Captains must give the appearance of standing in support of one another so that dissent does not flourish in the lower ranks. The seeds of mutiny are so easily grown during difficult times at sea. Unfortunately, I have let my true feelings slip often enough that Benwick, sharp as he is, can have little trouble in guessing them.

What occurred is this: we had safely delivered our convoy to port in India and were resupplied and back out to sea very quickly. I was not sad at this, as it is the summer and the mainland is rife with sickness at the moment. The only unfortunate development was that Captain Austen was reassigned and I was once again left alone in the company of Captain Fowler. You can imagine the disappointment I felt at losing the HMS *St Albans* and the intelligent discourse of her captain.

We were back out to sea and on our way once again to China to escort ships back towards the west. A

French merchant frigate was spotted in the distance, and I merely glanced over at the *Mandy*, assuming that she would be under the guidance of First Lieutenant Harville. To my utter amazement, Captain Fowler himself stood the decks and was giving the order to run up the flag to give chase. I was so shocked that I had to inspect the deck of the *Mandy* closer with my spyglass.

We set sail. I gave the order to clear the deck for action, and the distance between us and the merchant ship closed rapidly. It was nothing unusual in the battle itself. Both *Mandy* and *Laconia* gave passing broadsides. The frigate returned fire in a half-hearted manner, knowing that it was destined for capture and wanting to sustain as few deaths and injuries as possible. Captain Fowler did an admirable job, and nothing was wanting in the direction he gave to his ship and men.

After our quarry ran up their white flag of surrender, *Mandy* drifted farther from the French frigate than was usual. So I gave the order for men from *Laconia* to board and capture the crew of the frigate. Once all was settled on the captured ship, Benwick brought my attention to the flag that *Mandy* had run up requesting me to come aboard. After giving the order for our launch to be put in the water, I peered through my spyglass at *Mandy*. There was an unusual grouping and activity on deck.

'What do you make of it, Benwick?'

'I can't say, sir. Nothing beyond very minimal damage seems apparent on the decks. I can't imagine they sustained enough damage to warrant assistance.'

I made ready to leave and gave command to Benwick until my return, then climbed down into the boat and was rowed over, grumbling to myself at the damned inconvenience of it.

Once on deck of the *Mandy*, a pale-faced Harville came up and saluted me.

'It's Captain Fowler, sir. He's dead.'

I was expecting to be led to Fowler's cabin and showed the body laid out with his life's blood pooling beneath him. But no—Harville took me to the fore of the ship, and there he lay, with absolutely not a single drop of blood taken from his body, looking very much as he always did, except sober. The ship's doctor stood over him, looked up, and shook his head.

'He's dead, sir.'

Now Anne, you know that the death of a captain, especially one as disliked as Fowler, is a very serious matter. It was imperative that I completely ruled out murder. As much for the sake of the memory of Fowler as for the reputation of all who served under him.

I turned to Harville. 'What in God's name killed him? I see no injury to his body.'

'Well, sir,' Harville stuttered out, 'that cannon there.' He gestured to a deck cannon that was pointing the wrong way and on its side beside Fowler. 'It rose up and over and came down directly on top of Captain Fowler as he stood behind it.'

'Are you certain? Had it been properly secured before battle so the recoil would not kill anyone?'

'Yes, sir! It was very properly secured. It was not the recoil. The entire cannon lifted and flipped over and on him, sir. Pardon my saying so, but I have never seen anything like it before.'

'Was the cannon being shot?'

'No, sir. It had just been shot, and the gun crew

manning it were preparing to reload it when there was a bang and it rose up and overturned.'

'Where is your armourer?'

'Mr Bottles! Step forward!' Harville called.

An older man many times at sea stepped forward, wringing his hat and offering a most improbable explanation I could scarce believe.

'I never seen it happen before, but I've heard that another cannonball entering the mouth of the cannon after it was discharged could cause it to act so. It would be an almost impossible shot, but perhaps that is what happened, sir.'

After much inspection, Bottles removed the entire firing mechanism of the cannon and peered into the end of it farthest from the opening. There, in the end, was a cannonball shot from the French frigate that had entered with such force that it was melted to the inside. The cannon had broken its rigging and flipped up into the air and onto poor Fowler. There was barely a scratch upon him, but he was surely killed almost instantly.

Indeed, when I recorded the incredible incident into the ship's log, I was able to give the very second he died, for Fowler had on his person a very handsome pocket watch that recorded the very moment of his passing by the face and hands of it being crushed permanently into the position of the time of the accident. Anne, it was one of those incredible things that, had I not been there to see it for myself, I would hardly have been able to believe it.

I turned to Harville. The good man had composed himself admirably; only the slight pallor of his face gave any sign of a recent shock.

'Mr Harville, you are now acting captain of the

HMS *Mandy*. I will make a note of it in the ship's log of the *Laconia*. You are to do the same for the ship's log of the *Mandy*.'

I could see this was most definitely not the way that Harville had anticipated he would gain his first command of a ship. There are many heartless, ambitious first lieutenants who would delight in attaining a promotion by any means necessary. And although I can be quite certain that Captain Fowler created an enormous amount of strain for the nerves of Harville, I am sure he would not have had it this way for the world.

When I climbed the ladder back into the launch still bobbing alongside *Mandy*, my men looked at me, burning with curiosity. But no one said a word. Later, I informed Benwick of what had occurred.

'Benwick, if I had not seen it with my own eyes… It was a one in a million shot, pure chance.'

'Yes, sir. Perhaps more was at work than what is found solely in the providence of chance.'

'Belay that talk, Benwick. I will not stand for any mutterings among the men of the Hand of God or anything of the like. You and I may very well share those opinions, but we keep them to ourselves.'

'Understood, sir.'

And so concludes the ignominious career of Captain Fowler. I feel a burden has been lifted, I am sorry to say. I know you would be perfectly correct in all that you would have to say to chastise me for this feeling, but I cannot help it, not when the lives of so many men were in the hands of such a wastrel—not to mention the families and children of the men back on shore!

No, Anne, I realise it shows me in an inglorious

light, but I cannot pretend to regret the truly bizarre accident that took Fowler's life. I do not rejoice in it, but the immediate benefits are palpable. The men are in the much more steady, capable hands of Harville now. And, to the benefit of Fowler's prestigious family, he will be recorded as having died in battle, on deck and somewhat sober. It will not be my duty to record him fading away in his bunk, sodden to the core with strong spirits. Forgive me for my cold heart.

I am afraid I will never attain that magnanimous, Christian compassion that you dispense with such ease. How you were always able to find the sometimes very minute kernel of good in all those around you and celebrate it while acknowledging their failings with a truthful eye, I will never know. You have a bold, strong heart, Anne, and I like to think that I am a much better man for having known you. I wonder if you can say the same? I cannot claim to possess your goodness of spirit, but I hope you feel your life is richer as a consequence of our short, too short, time together.

Your Obedient Servant,
Captain Frederick Wentworth
HMS Laconia

Despite the very real danger Captain Fowler put my husband and his own men through, I could not help but feel a tear run down my cheek for him. Frederick had told me a little of him and all the attendant anxiety that came from being sent on assignments with him, but he had always quickly brushed over Fowler's death as having happened during battle with no further embellishment. He had only mentioned in passing that Fowler had, on occasion, indulged in his cups to excess.

I, too, had changed since my first encounter with Frederick. In the time that followed, I looked with an honest eye at my fault of giving credence to the opinions of others over my own well-reasoned conclusions. Seeing his bold spirit and loving it with all my heart had given me the courage to embrace, in my own quiet way, an inner strength that I had not known had been there. Loving Frederick Wentworth had made me a better person, even if providence had not seen fit to reunite us. If there had been no four-day storm to greet him when he returned to Plymouth on the *Asp* after his first year as a captain, if he had indeed ridden to Kellynch Hall the night of his arrival and begged me to be his wife again, I would have possessed the strength of spirit to have given him an unequivocal yes.

When Claire joined me later that morning, I silently mused whether the attachment between her and young Charles was a renewal of sentiments that lingered from childhood or if it was a freshly formed bloom. She had asked me to tell her my remembrances of nursing him as a very young invalid and listened with rapt attention. I looked up at her as her fine long neck craned once again towards the window, brows furrowed at the frustrating oak leaves that impeded a perfect view. She looked so young! But, I told myself with a wry smile, she was just over a year younger than I was when I lost my heart to Frederick.

Had I really been so very young? No wonder Lady Russell had felt the need to counsel me with such determination against the idea of marrying and perhaps travelling across the world far from friends and family with a penniless, young captain. I would not advise the same as she, but looking at Claire, so young and hopeful, I had more clarity and more understanding in my heart as to Lady Russell's motives.

Finally, a rattle of wheels could be distinguished and she jumped up, wringing her hands and arranging her already perfect curls. At that very moment, I felt a twinge that spread and then receded from my belly and I became lost in my own thoughts, while Claire was bundled up and whisked off to Uppercross.

Needing movement, I got up and walked around the room. Suddenly, our airy bedroom felt too tight, too small. I rang for Maude and, when she hurried in, placed my hand on her forearm, asking her to send word to Mr Falgarth.

She turned to leave before I halted her movement again. "And Maude, regardless of my condition, please inform me at any time of Captain Wentworth's arrival."

CHAPTER EIGHTEEN

The next two days were a trial that confronted all the strength of my soul and body. My confinement with Freddie had been so uneventful, so quick, that this difficulty surprised me. I made it through and was rewarded with a very thin cry from my surprisingly small child.

Maude presented me with the pale, perfect face of my daughter, swaddled tightly against the sudden chills of an early spring. She nursed very quietly and with earnest focus on my breast. Once, her wide eyes opened to study me for just a moment with all the wisdom of the ages twinkling in them. Despite my weariness, I smiled back at the dear one and wished with all my heart that Frederick were there to greet his little girl. We both closed our eyes for a long and deep sleep.

When I awoke, I saw a figure sitting by the window, indistinct, blue, large. My eyes opened wider to see Frederick bathed in the dim light of dawn, holding our daughter close to his chest. His blue captain's jacket was crusted over with salt in patches, indicating that he had been bracing himself on the deck of his ship in some of the bitterest weather that the Irish Sea and St George's Channel could throw at him. His face was dark from a beard that had gone several days without the benefit of a razor.

He must have ridden day and night to return, not pausing at an inn between here and Portsmouth for a shave and sleep. My heart swelled to see him cooing some soft, lilting nonsense down into the face of our little girl. His eyes rose and met mine. Warmth of love and gratitude spread across his chiselled, rugged face. His eyes glistened as he blinked rapidly.

"Here now, Anne. Did you give permission for this stow-away to board our ship?" He smiled rakishly as he stood and walked over softly, not daring to jostle the baby with movement too sudden.

"I am afraid I did."

"Well, we can overlook it this time and give her permission to stay aboard, what say you?"

He sat gingerly on the edge of the bed.

"I am in full agreement, Captain Wentworth."

He leant over and kissed me softly on the forehead and then on both cheeks. "Was it a hard time?"

I nodded, but then, eager to forget and hear of his voyage, asked, "Did you have a difficult time of it? The ship on Tuskar Rock?"

His face clouded a little. "Yes, the da—" He cleared his throat. "The deuced thing broke free as we waited for a reprieve from the weather and ran aground in Rosslare Harbour! The weather barely gave us a chance to secure the ship, but we managed to tow her into Wexford. If I never see the HMS *Bellona* again, it will be far too soon. She had a...a decided dislike to the entire undertaking, and we were fortunate enough to accomplish our mission without the *Stoic* being dragged onto the rocks by her!"

I smiled at each pause in his speech, knowing it usually required several days of onshore life to lessen Frederick's habit of using the coarse language he sometimes employed while at sea.

"I am sorry that *Bellona* was not more cooperative, dear. But your new ship, the HMS *Stoic*? Did she handle herself well?"

To Frederick's eye came that dreamy look he would get when he spoke of a ship for which he had a special affinity.

"Like a song, Anne. You will love her as I do, I am sure. During the worst that the Irish Sea could throw at any man, she remained steady and true."

"If you love her and she delivered you safely back to me, she already has my deepest regards."

He looked down at the baby he still held. "Our daughter, what are we to christen her?" He dropped a light kiss on the baby's forehead. "A stunning beauty like her needs a memorable name, yes?"

"What of Nelly? In honour of Lord Nelson."

"Hmm, Nelly Anne Wentworth? I must say it has a musical lilt that I find very pleasing."

"Anne?"

"Yes. In honour of another brave soul whom I admire very much indeed."

I smiled up at him. Despite my exhaustion, I could not help but take advantage of a minor ruse of my own. Frederick was always the one having fun with a good tease; I certainly ought to have one too on the rare occasions when I thought of it.

"But, then again, Frederick, what is your opinion of the name Hazel?"

Frederick frowned down at little Nelly Anne and then looked back up at me.

"Hazel? It is a good name, but is there someone in your family that goes by it? I do not recall hearing it before."

"You do not recall the import of Hazel? Indeed, Frederick, you astonish me! How can you so easily forget that speech you gave to Louisa Musgrove? We were on a long walk, and you told her to allow nothing to change her mind and keep herself firm in all things, just as a hazelnut. You even lifted one to show her the model of perfection of which you spoke. And if I recall, the main point of your argument was that she should strive to be 'in possession of all the happiness that a hazelnut can be supposed capable of.'"

"Good God, you heard that ridiculous little speech? I gave it in jest! You heard me prattle away like that and never told me all these years? Why, you sly thing!"

"It was quite by accident that I overheard. If I had been a part of the discussion, I would have pointed out the very obvious flaw in your logic that should the hazelnut never allow itself to change and be influenced by forces greater than itself, such as rain and sun, it will never grow into the lovely little tree it has the potential to be. By extending itself, it may experience even greater happiness than it can know as a hazelnut. In order to become greater than our present selves, we must yield a bit of our guard and allow our shell to crack and dissipate."

Frederick laughed and looked down at the babe in his arms. "And that is why you never attempt to win an argument against your mother, dear girl. Remember this lesson well, Nelly Anne Hazel Wentworth!"

The baby let out a gurgle, as if to demonstrate her agreement in the entire matter.

"Frederick, I was joking!" I said, laughing.

"No, no, Anne! It is all too late! You just saw with your own eyes how much she approves of the name Hazel being added. Nelly Anne Hazel Wentworth is in full agreement. Too late to change course now!"

"Frederick, you are the most infuriating man I have ever met!"

"I know," he said with his boyish smile lighting its way through that handsome, bearded, tired face of his.

CHAPTER NINETEEN

May 1825

J ust over a year after our daughter was born, Captain
Wentworth was assigned to the Port of Bridgetown,
Barbados in the West Indies. We were to regretfully
leave our sweet little manor house in Somersetshire for
a time. Betsy and Jim were to stay on at the house and keep it
in good repair for our eventual return to England. It was no
small feat to organise and pack up our belongings, but the
clothing, foods, and comforts of home were items that I
could easily forgo in order to accompany Frederick to the
ends of the earth. There were only ever two things that
spurred regret in my heart at the beginning of a long voyage
—my books and my piano.

My pianoforte, a gift from Frederick when we first set up
house in England after travels overseas, was in our parlour.
In terms of possessions, it was one of my greatest comforts
and joys. I would have had a miserable time trying to rank

which was of more value for my peaceable mind—my piano or my books.

After a long day of sorting and packing, I sat down at the pianoforte after Nelly Anne and Freddie had gone up to bed. I raised the lid and lightly ran my fingertips along the cool keys in silence. Pages of music rested on top of the instrument. I opened it and played softly, knowing the sound of loud music was a very justifiable excuse for children to leap out of bed and noisily stomp down stairs. But Freddie was so excited about the impending sea voyage that he wore himself out thoroughly almost daily. Especially so that day because Frederick had arrived home after preparing the *Stoic* as fully as possible before he loaded up his family for the trip across the Atlantic.

I heard my husband walk up behind me. He placed one hand on my shoulder, his thumb and first two fingers warm as they gently caressed my neck. I leant my cheek down to press onto his hand while I continued to play. A smile that was unseen by him spread across my lips as I told myself there could be no greater happiness than this moment.

"You will miss it terribly, will you not, Anne? Your lovely piano."

"Oh, I can overcome any trial at sea, as long as I am at your side and our children are happy and well. There is little else I desire, as you know."

He leant down and gave a ticklish kiss to that spot where neck and shoulder meet. I hit a note wrong and laughed.

"You have made me spoil my sonata."

"But for the best of reasons," he said as he delivered several more kisses to my neck.

He sat next to me, with his back to the instrument.

"But truly, Anne, you would be happier if you had a way to play music once we reach the West Indies, would you not?"

"I am happiest when our family is together. But I would be untruthful if I were to say that music is not very important to me. To both of us, I think."

"Yes, who else swells my voice as well as you, Anne? None. You know how much I love to hear myself sing! You must have an instrument in Barbados."

"But it would be such an inconvenience to transport this pianoforte on a journey such as this! I should think the room can hardly be spared. Especially now since we have the belongings of two children to consider as well."

"You are correct, but"—he drew a paper out of a side pocket—"I happen to have several possibilities we can explore with those who may have a clue as to where we can lay our hands on a small, square piano left there a few years ago by a friend of Admiral Croft. It should still be somewhere on the island or nearby. I have already sent a dispatch to the West Indies to ferret out its current location. With a little luck, we can track it down once we get settled."

"Oh, that would be wonderful!" I threw my arms around his neck and hugged him close, then pulled away to admire his neat list. "This is so thoughtful of you, Frederick."

"Anything for you, love. You will have two small children to manage. If this is something that can give you comfort during your quiet hours, or minutes I should say, it would be well worth the exertion. So be sure to make a sliver of space available to stow away a few sheets of music."

"Any requests?"

"Well, you must include several songs that absolutely require a booming, baritone voice of superior quality from a handsome man."

"But where shall I find such a person? I would think such a man does not exist," I stated, wide-eyed and innocent.

Frederick gave me a tight squeeze and another kiss on the neck until my laughter rang through the room. A muffled fuss of the baby was heard, and I rushed off to calm the child awakened by our foolish teasing.

Once aboard the HMS *Stoic* and on our way across the Atlantic, it took very little time for the children to adapt to life aboard a ship. Freddie was barefoot and trying out his climbing skills in the shrouds for much of the days and seeking out the camaraderie of some of the ship's boys, the youngest of these fellows being a ten-year-old who took a liking to him.

Nelly Anne smiled more in the first week aboard HMS *Stoic* than I had ever seen before. It was on the swaying quarterdeck that she clung to my skirts, stood with determination, and tottered her first steps just behind the wheel of the ship. Her grasping little hand clutched at the base of the wheel to steady herself, causing the quartermaster who was steering to grin down at her in admiration.

"Such steady sea legs, Miss Nelly!" he exclaimed.

Nelly grinned up into his wizened face, a rare smile to a stranger.

I was delighted to be back at sea, surrounded once more by the wooden world of life aboard a ship. After too long on dry land, there was a spring in my step when I saw the sails lifted aloft and the wind filled them readily.

CHAPTER TWENTY

We arrived in Barbados without anything more dramatic to report than the very first steps of Nelly Anne. The event did not make it into the official ship's log, but it was thoroughly discussed by the entire crew who took a measure of personal pride in the event.

Just outside the city of Bridgetown, we pulled up to a very fine, small white house set among lush foliage. Frederick had secured it by his winning ways with his superiors, and I was pleased to be in a smaller port town where the social demands for a captain's wife would be less severe.

A bead of sweat trickled down my spine, reminding me of the unforgiving warmth there. Our two tired children were unloaded by myself and Maude and carried into the house. Frederick was to remain on the *Stoic* with the purser for the rest of the day to oversee the organisation of resupplying such a large ship.

"Well, Maude, what say you to our new manor house?" I whispered as we made our way through the front door.

"It reminds me very much of some of the white houses near the quay in Lyme. Only flatter and more porches sticking out from it along the side. Like a giant spider squatted down with porches for legs."

"Yes, I suppose you are right," I said with a quiet laugh.

We settled in nicely and quite gorged ourselves on the fresh fruit awaiting us. It raised my energy after the stale foods of the crossing. I marvelled at how quickly Maude took to trying several unusual fruits. She never ceased to surprise me with how easily acclimated she became in the most unfamiliar circumstances.

Frederick arrived home with his face clearly showing the strain of docking a large ship, organising replenishment of the stores, and finalising leave for the men to ensure few desertions. A quiet dinner took place that evening as the children accustomed themselves to flooring that did not shift underfoot. To our great amusement, dear Nelly Anne seemed to be having a more difficult time walking on land than she did at sea.

"She is not a landlubber, I see!" Frederick exclaimed as he caught her hand in an unsteady moment. Nelly Anne snatched it away and continued her wobbly course solo with a defiant look at her father.

"The spirit of Lord Nelson! She will be a strong and capable one, Anne."

"Yes. I believe you are correct on that point, Frederick." I smiled at my girl as she reached a chubby hand up to a plate of mango on the table and swayed precariously. I inched the plate closer to her hand, but offered no other interference to the iron-willed little one.

"Papa! How about me?" Freddie was not to be outdone by his little sister. "Did you see my quickest time in the shrouds? Jody said I was the fastest son of an officer he had ever seen! I almost beat him the day we made port."

"I think it may have been a naval record for a lad your age. You proved yourself to be a very worthy addition to the crew and a credit to the navy during our voyage."

Freddie's chest puffed up so much, the front of his shirt dabbed into the sauce on the edge of his dinner plate. I was too amused to scold him about the stain, secretly thankful that our voyage had been so pleasant and easy. If the worst to show for it were some missed lessons and stained shirts, I was very grateful indeed.

"Anne," Frederick said as he leant back, "I have discovered today that the square piano that was once here at this harbour has somehow made its way to Port of Spain in Trinidad. It is on the mainland and a mere day and a half of sailing from here."

"Is there any ship likely to be going there soon?" I asked eagerly.

"In fact, a frigate is scheduled to travel there in a week. It is captained by a young whip named William Price, lately made a master and commander, this being his first posting. I have sent a letter to him asking about the possibility of including your square piano in with the other supplies of food and gunpowder he will be bringing back from Port of Spain."

"Oh Frederick!" I said, laying a hand on his forearm. "With all your worries of *Stoic*, you found time to settle this matter as well? You are too good to me! But, will it be too much to ask of Price?"

"Not at all! All these freshly made young men want to impress the likes of the famous and dashing Captain Wentworth. And, more importantly, they especially want him to pass along a good word to his brother-in-law Admiral Croft."

"Or," I felt compelled to point out, "Captain Price is

simply a kind young man, happy to be of service where he can be."

"Yes, Anne, that too."

"If you have no objection, Frederick, I will go with the ship to personally thank the mistress of the house the piano has resided in. I hope she experiences no discomfort at its loss."

"No, as far as I can make out, it has been consigned to a little guest house and risks rotting away from disuse. It is behind the governor's residence there, so you will no doubt have to spend some time chatting with his wife about the latest news from England. I know your aversion to gossip, so that should be payment enough. Look here, Anne, must you go and see to this personally?"

"Yes, if Captain Price has no objection, I will go attend to it myself. I know very well that he will be busy safely loading cargo onto his ship and keeping his men from drinking to excess on shore. And I wish to thank Lady Woodford personally for the lend of the instrument. A piano in this part of the world is so very rare, I feel I must visit with her and, at the very least, tell her the latest news from home."

"Well, if you are certain, I am sure he will have little objection."

In another week, after I was satisfied with the running of our new house and the hiring of a few locals to help Maude with whatever may arise, I prepared myself for the very brief voyage to Port of Spain to collect the piano. We had left an open place in the parlour for the precious instrument. A small trunk was all I needed and, of course, one book would suffice to get me to and from the mainland. Such a quick voyage required very little luggage.

Frederick walked the length of the HMS *Lucille* along the dock, from bow to stern and back again, maintaining a professional dignity in his bearing the entire time. Finally, he paused before me, hands clasped behind his back with one leg forward, looking the very picture of Royal Navy strength. His tall bearing, so inconvenient in the small cabins of a ship and the source of many a tender forehead from unexpected bumps, looked imposing on this sunny, warm day on the dock.

Standing before me, he said, "Ready for your voyage, Mrs Wentworth?"

"Very ready, Captain Wentworth. I believe this will be one of the very few times I have been aboard a ship without your company. An adventure of my own, so to speak."

"Yes. I have not yet seen Captain Price in action, as he is newly made, but I hear very good things of him. He sounds like a very capable young man who rose through the ranks mostly due to the distinction of his character in action."

"His young wife seemed a very kind, well-spoken young lady when we met for tea last week. Frederick, Maude has hired a local wet nurse for Nelly Anne and a few day maids, but should anything occur to me—"

"Nothing will occur to you, Anne! These waters are well patrolled. We are at peace with France. It is only because the French are still in possession of the islands of Guadeloupe and Martinique that the Admiralty wants to maintain a strong naval presence in this part of the world. There is little in the Caribbean Seas to threaten these days."

I knew this little speech of Frederick's was to stave off his own anxieties rather than to lessen any of mine, which were minimal. Truthfully, after the stresses of moving a family from England to the Windward Islands—having to corral a small child just learning to walk on the deck of a swaying ship, always looking upward into the shrouds for signs that little Frederick was still well and uninjured—the thought of a few nights alone in the cabin of a ship was a welcome change. As much as I adored my children and husband, I was feeling worn thin.

I laid my hand on Frederick's forearm, looking deep into his eyes. "Should anything occur to delay my return, Captain Price's wife, Mrs Sara Price, has made the very generous offer of her services to aid Maude in the running of the house. As you say, she seems a very capable young woman, from a seagoing family that hails from Bigbury-on-Sea, near Plymouth. She had an active hand in helping her mother to raise a large family of ten children. Please do not hesitate to call upon her, Frederick."

Those dark eyes of his gazed into mine, causing the rise of a very familiar, but always welcome, flutter of my heart. He leant in and kissed me quickly, unconcerned as to who may see from the dock or ships.

"I shall see you settled, if that is permitted, Mrs Wentworth."

I smiled up at him. "You have permission to come aboard, Captain Wentworth."

We both walked onto the deck of the *Lucille*, and Frederick did a thorough walk around the cabin that Captain Price had abandoned for a few days in concession to my comfort and convenience. When the tide turned, Frederick returned to the dock and stood stock-still, watching while the *Lucille* glided away.

As the ship set sail from Bridgetown harbour, I keenly watched Frederick from the bulwarks as he stood motionless on the dock, bidding me farewell with his heart, but not his hand. I had no need for professional decorum and raised my hand to bid him farewell. Perhaps the strong sun was playing with my imagination, but I seemed to see a grin steal across his lips. The shore of Barbados receded as the wind set us on our way.

CHAPTER TWENTY-ONE

Since we made dock early in the morning, Captain Price had informed me that we may make the tide to leave in the late afternoon and spend but one night at sea. I understood what was left unsaid by him, that he hoped that I would attend to the frivolous business of retrieving my square piano so that he may get back as soon as possible. Thus, when we landed at the Port of Spain in Trinidad, I quickly left the *Lucille* and hired a respectable-looking cart and driver to take me to the residence that held the musical instrument. It was a small cottage that stood behind the Government House on Belmont Hill, the residence of the Governor of Trinidad.

I was greeted by the governor's wife, Lady Woodford, an older lady with an ample personage and a slightly fretful manner. With minimal reluctance, I accepted her invitation to join her for tea, knowing she would scavenge as much recent news from England as she could get from me. I imagined how this would be a great source of comfort for her in the coming days when she could tell and retell all to her

social circle. Caution and neutrality of feeling were imperative so that some slight observational opinion was not trans-
formed by embellishment to a full-blown tale of malicious
gossip. My compassion for her situation overcame my
natural inclination to avoid the rather tedious minutiae of
idle talk, and I settled in for a chat.

After my third cup of tea, I leant slightly to notice the
slant of the sun cast down from the palm trees in front of the
house. I cleared my throat when Lady Woodford began a
nostalgic waxing on the architecture of her childhood estate.

"Lady Woodford, if I may, I see by the shadows of the sun
that the day wears on. I am aware that Captain Price wishes
to leave on the late tide, if possible."

A bustle of activities ensued, and with a few pleasantries
and directions to the servants as to the proper way to load
the square box piano onto the cart, Lady Woodford waved
goodbye as the cart wound its way down the hill.

Once back at the dock, the men from the HMS *Lucille*
loaded my little treasure into the cabin and stowed it under
the bed that I would be sleeping in. Since it was a small
square piano with legs that were detached, it fit well enough
for such a quick voyage. A few times, I heard the tinkle of
chords when the handling of the instrument was less than
careful.

My fingers itched to play the keys of the instrument
stowed beneath my berth, but I forced myself to be content
with the book I had brought as companionship.

In the middle of the calm, quiet night, a cry shattered my
sleep. I awoke fully, still in that special state of all mothers
who respond unconsciously to the slightest disturbance in
the night, although my children were many miles from me. I
paused and heard nothing but a very gentle lap of waves.
Thinking my anxiety from being far from my family the

cause of a runaway imagination, I began to settle back down in my berth.

A cry reached my ears again, this time unmistakably real and very close by. I heard footfalls and perhaps some mutterings as well. My hand extended out for my robe and shawl to cover my nightgown as I rose from bed. I crept to the door of the small cabin and waited, with one hand resting on the wood. My whole focus was turned to my ears as they strained to pick up the slightest hint as to what was transpiring on the ship.

Another ship attacking would have resulted in an enormous fit of noisy boots on the deck, piping to arms, the thunderous rolling out of the cannons, and shouted orders. None of those sounds came to my ears.

A mutiny? It was still too quiet for such a possibility. The men aboard the *Lucille* seemed as content a lot of officers and seamen as I had witnessed anywhere before. My hand moved to the lock of the door.

Do not be foolish, Anne. Stay where you are and be safe. I could hear Frederick's voice in my mind. Usually, in all things of the sea, I would defer to his judgment. But curiosity overcame my memory of his advice through the years.

Another cry of pain and fear from the same voice decided for me. I gently unbolted and opened the door. I proceeded down the hatch to the gun deck of the ship where the hammocks of the men were slung up over the cannons that were ready to be rolled up to the gunports at a moment's notice. Many men were gathered around one hammock, including the ship's doctor and Captain Price.

A young man, an officer by the looks of him, was writhing in his hammock. A sheen of sweat coated his face. He could not be much more than eighteen years of age. I reached out past the men and took his hand in mine.

Another seaman was coating his brow with cool water. Price turned to me, his young brow furrowed in concern.

"Mrs Wentworth, you should not be down here, ma'am. It is Midshipman Ross. He may have the yellow fever."

"What are his symptoms?"

"He woke suddenly with chills and fever, and his body aches all over. You should return to your cabin to be safe."

"Captain Price, I do appreciate your concern, however, I have already experienced yellow fever on a previous voyage, and therefore, I believe I am unlikely to experience it again. Mr Cole, I have some skill in nursing the sick and injured, so will you please notify me if you think I could be of service in any way?"

"Yes, ma'am."

After seeing that the doctor was doing all he could to minister to the man, I turned to leave, knowing that my presence was causing the inexperienced young captain some anxiety. How could he return to port with a very senior captain's wife near death with a disease? At least he would be able to say that he had instructed me to stay away. His conscience and his reputation would be clear of any recrimination.

I lay in my berth that night with the restlessness of anxiety tearing away at me. Every time I felt the cabin was too stifling, I wondered if a fever was developing. Every time my body felt the need to shift positions, I suddenly awakened to wonder if the early stages of aches were beginning. Then, of course, the thoughts of what would become of my family ran circles through my mind. I was grateful for the few hours of sleep that I did manage to achieve before I saw the soft glow of morning on the eastern horizon through the window. I felt tired as I rose, but knew it was from an unsettled mind rather than any physical ailment. If the rest of the ship was feeling well, that might mean that poor Midshipman Ross was but an isolated case.

As I prepared to leave my cabin, I could hear the rhythmic whooshing sound of the ship's pumps being worked. Captain Price was clearly taking no chances. The bilge water in the hold was being pulled up and expelled from the ship to be replaced by a fresh batch of water. It showed an initiative to not take the health of his men lightly, as some captains did.

A whiff of smoke reached my nose. But instead of the usual panic from imagining a burning ship sinking into the sea, I reassured myself that the lower decks were being smoked to decrease the possibility of an infection spreading.

On deck, I approached Captain Price.

"How is the sick man doing this morning, sir?"

"Not well, I'm afraid. Mr Cole believes it is yellow fever. While we loaded the supplies on board, Ross had several errands to run in a part of the town that is known to be a haven of stagnant waters. The doctor has informed me that it may be likely that he became sick there."

"Then there is a chance the rest of the crew might be spared?"

"Yes, there is a chance. Most of us have visited the Windward Islands before and have already endured yellow fever. My first visit in this part of the world saw a quarter of the crew fall deadly ill and at least a dozen buried. I hope that will not be the case in this instance."

"Yes, let us hope dearly, Captain."

"I regret to inform you that, once we reach Bridgetown, I shall have to raise the double yellow jack."

I blew out a heavy breath, knowing that this trip might be much longer than originally anticipated. Once near port in Barbados, two yellow flags would be run up to indicate that illness was on board and we would need to be cleared before docking.

"I think it has been a long while since Barbados has experienced yellow fever, so they will be cautious when it comes to us." Price looked down apologetically as he said this, as if regretting having to inform me. I could not help but smile at him being so self-conscious in my presence.

"I have been through similar experiences, Captain Price. I appreciate you keeping me informed and am ready to offer my services in any way that would help."

CHAPTER TWENTY-TWO

As we sailed back to Barbados, the wind and current were against us. Thus, it took longer on the return journey than the one that went out. It was late the next morning when we sighted land.

Our boat was visible to the harbour when Price ordered the raising of the two yellow flags. I looked up at them whipping in the wind, the innocent little sheets of fabric announcing to the world that this ship could be a bringer of death. If Frederick was on the deck of the HMS *Stoic*, his spyglass would reveal our ship and the little flags that attended it. I shook my head as I imagined his anxiety when he viewed the double yellow jack. If I saw such a thing on his ship after a voyage, my mind would leap to the worst conclusions. Poor Frederick.

As we neared land, a longboat was rowing out to meet us from the shore. Another longboat had been put to the water from the *Stoic* and was also rowing towards us. I saw Frederick standing in the bow of that boat as it neared. If willpower could propel a ship, that little longboat would have been flying through the water.

Once the boat with the government officials was close to us, a shouted conversation through speaking trumpets took place between Captain Price, Mr Cole, and the land officials. It was decided that we would be quarantined for at least a se'nnight, if no additional crewmen became ill. If more became ill, we would need to stay on the ship for two weeks or longer. The conversation was so bellowed, it left no one aboard *Lucille* in doubt of their fate for the next fortnight. A few groans escaped from the mouths of several men.

"Belay that talk, men! Get back to your stations!" Price snapped.

The anticipated boredom undoubtedly made their hearts heavy. We were more than amply supplied with food from our trip to Trinidad. Stacks of chickens in cages were stuffed behind the wheel of the ship. The hold had barrels of fresh foods intended for the ships in port at Bridgetown. Anything that was lacking would be sent out to us and hoisted on board.

"You may wish to request extra food for the chickens, Captain Price," I muttered in as quiet and unobtrusive a voice as I could manage.

He nodded a curt response and bellowed as much to the men in the bobbing vessel below. By then, Frederick's boat had arrived and his worried face peered up at the railing of the ship. I waved at him with a broad smile on my face, hoping to reassure him of my health and happiness. He waved me to the ship's bow and barked some orders to his men. We met in a place where our shouting could not be heard over all the other shouting going on.

"Anne! Are you well? Are you certain?"

"Yes, I am well. It is one man who has contracted yellow

fever or malaria. I think the rest of us may be out of danger, as no one else has exhibited any symptoms."

"Can I bring you anything to help you pass the time?"

"Some of my books, please. You know my tastes and what I love best. You may also bring some sheets of music, for it seems I shall have an abundance of time with my lovely instrument!"

The lines of worry smoothed from his face when he broke out in a hearty laugh. Then, likely recalling his boat full of men waiting at their oars, he made his face impassive again.

"Yes, well. Very good, Mrs Wentworth. I shall be certain to deliver those items you requested to you tomorrow, as soon as may be. Until tomorrow, then."

I yearned to ask of the children, but I knew how seriously Frederick viewed his professional deportment in front of his men. If anything had arisen with Nelly Anne and Freddie, I was certain he would have told me.

True to his word, Frederick had his men row him over from the HMS *Stoic* almost at daybreak.

At the bow of the ship, I leant over and smiled down upon him. He smiled up at me, his handsome face ruddy in the reddish light of dawn.

"I trust you are in good health, madam?" he asked rakishly.

"Very good health, sir. Thank you so very much for your kind inquiry. And how do you and your family fare on this fine day?"

"Very well. Thank you for your equally kind inquiry. Such gracious manners are rarely to be encountered. Though, I must confess a resident at my home is more fractious than is commonly encountered in one with such a small frame. A certain Miss N. A. Hazel Wentworth has voiced some rather robust protestations about how things are done at our establishment. She can be very constant in her observations, do you not find, madam?"

"I hear she is particularly fond of mangoes, sir. That may cool her temperament."

"Ah! Thank you, Mrs Wentworth."

"Not at all, Captain Wentworth." I could not help but giggle at such a ridiculously formal exchange.

"As a token of my appreciation, allow me to send up a parcel for you to peruse at your leisure."

"You are kindness itself, sir."

One of the crew came over and caught the rope that was tossed up. A tightly wrapped bundle swung free from Frederick's boat and made its way on board the ship. I held it to my chest and gazed at my husband.

"Until we meet again, madam."

"Yes, I look forward to it with all my heart, sir."

He gave a slight bow, half serious, half in jest. His crew began the trip back to *Stoic*, and we both watched each other until we lost sight.

With a sigh, I untied the package back in the cabin. I was sadly aware that my presence meant that poor Captain Price had to stay bunked up with his first lieutenant. My silly encounter with Frederick had cheered me. If everyone was still in good health that afternoon, I intended to ask the captain if he would grant permission for some of the men to set up the square piano on the deck somewhere.

When the oilskin cloth fell away, I found a bundle of letters tied with a red ribbon, a packet of some sort, and two additional letters on top of a stack of books. With a gasp, I realised the bundle with the red ribbon was another set of letters addressed to me that Frederick had written during his eight years at sea after our broken engagement. The previous set, which I finished just before the birth of Nelly Anne, had brought me such joy during the worry of a difficult pregnancy. In the time afterwards, recovering my strength and looking after my dear children had consumed my attention so thoroughly that I had completely forgotten to ask Frederick if he had additional letters for me. Of course he did. That mischievous man. And now I had another set to distract me in a time of trial.

After hugging the bundle to my chest as a child might clutch a favourite toy, I picked up the other letters. One was from my sister Mrs Mary Musgrove of Uppercross. It must have arrived in a recent mailbag from England. The other was recently written by Frederick himself. I eagerly opened that one first.

Dearest Anne,

The children are well, but asking for you. I write this in the predawn hours before I am to leave our home, return to the ship, and row out to meet you with a package. I have hardly slept a wink for worry. If I find you still well in the morning, then I shall be easier in my mind, for it will be unlikely that yellow fever will get to you then. Perhaps I will rest easier tomorrow evening. A letter from your sister Mary will no doubt brighten your spirits and health, especially if she has much to say of her own ailments.

Included in this packet is a small bundle of herbs. Mr Dash, a physician here on this island for many years, says the locals use these particular herbs in a hot tea once a day to increase chances of survival from yellow fever. He also recommends fresh air and very minimal food, only liquids. I can procure more should you yourself have need of it, Anne. Mr Dash believes you to be safe from any serious case since you have had it before.

I also include the last, I swear to you the very last, bundle of those letters that I wrote to you during our time apart. I have not read them since they were sealed over ten years ago, so please forgive me if I said anything in anger or recorded events that may be shocking to you. This packet is smaller than the previous ones. I found that as the years went on, fewer were the times I wrote to you. It was not due to any lessening in affection for you, but a necessary step so that I might attempt to ease the sadness in my heart. Each letter I wrote to you brought you so vividly to my mind that I was low in spirits for several days afterwards. Regardless, I still found that I could not help but put pen to paper occasionally and unburden my heart to you in that open and free manner that we have always had. The more I saw of the world, the more I realised that it was so rare to encounter another one such as yourself with whom I had such a feeling of a kindred spirit. You see, some of your poetic nature has infected me over time. The letters lessened over those years, but my love did not. You will find my heart just as much yours as it has always been.

Please know that I shall think of you every moment of the day until you are safe in my arms again.

Yours, Entirely and Forever,

Captain Frederick Wentworth

HMS Stoic

To see the valediction of 'Yours, Entirely and Forever,' used again brought tears to my eyes. It was many minutes before I could put that letter down and turn over the packet of herbs with a calm and settled mind. Before anything else occurred, I must try to administer the tea to Midshipman Ross. Hopefully the doctor would see my offer in the light of helpfulness and not officiousness.

Mr Cole took no offence when I offered the warm cup of tea for Ross. His thoughts were that it was unlikely to have any truly beneficial effects, but little harm could come of it, so he raised no objection. I held the hand of Midshipman Ross for a time, speaking soothingly to his feverish face while I administered the herbal tea. It might have been imaginings of mine, but he seemed more at ease as he slipped into a calmer sleep.

CHAPTER TWENTY-THREE

Upon returning to my cabin, I picked up the letter from Mary. I had to pause and, since the gift of time was in ample supply at the moment, allow my mind to wander amusedly around the imaginings of what Mary's response would have been had she been required to be confined to a ship under the double yellow jack for a few weeks. There would not be enough cotton on this ship to stop up the ears of the crew against her loud complaints. I smiled and shook my head to dispel the image as I opened her letter. At least she did write to me when I was overseas, which was very kind of her.

Dear Anne.

How can you be so cruel as to be away from England at a time like this?

Against my express disapproval, our son Charles has announced his engagement to that girl, Claire Harville. Do you remember that you rid yourself of her presence when you had Nelly Anne a year ago? We were forced to have her over for what seemed like an eternity. She simply would not take the hint and leave. What ill-bred manners!

Of course, it did not help that my husband Charles kept asking her to extend her stay without first discussing it with me as he ought to have. I suspect that is when this terrible attachment first truly took root. I am supported by our father and Elizabeth in my condemnation of the engagement, but they refuse to leave Bath in order to make their views perfectly known to those here at Uppercross. Charles's mother does not share my dim view either. Her main concerns are limited to the venue of the dreaded event and what Claire Harville will wear. As if they could afford any truly quality fabric for her gown!

I am incensed, Anne, and feel entirely alone in my very proper objections to this match. I wish terribly that you were here to speak sense to my son and my husband! For reasons beyond me, they seem to truly listen to your counsel. It is very inconvenient that Frederick is constantly whisking you away to all ends of the earth, for in moments like this, when we should be united under the common interest of the respectability of the Elliot name, you are off pleasure-seeking in tropical climates.

It is highly inconvenient that Frederick should be so constantly answering to the demands of his profession. Is he not wealthy enough to retire? Or, surely, he should be made an admiral very soon, shan't he? Tell him what agonies I suffer when I alone am in England so valiantly upholding the Elliot legacy for future generations. Frederick's profession is a cruelty to me and an unnecessary hardship. The aches in my head that I have been subject to are beyond description, Anne. Please tell your husband that all of you should come back to England as soon as can be managed.

How are you doing? Very well, no doubt. Your health is always so robust. It is unfortunate that, among my sisters, I alone have been dealt the hand of poor health and weak nerves. Except for that time you imagined yourself feeling lowly when expecting Nelly Anne, you have always been so radiantly well. Even though I struggle with a delicate constitution, I possess a character that never seeks attention by announcing my hardships to the world and waving them about as if they were a flag.

I am indeed plagued by the most persistent pain in my side and throbbing of my temples ever since Charles gave his consent for this wretched engagement. It just may be the death of me! If only Charles and our son could realise the needless suffering they put me through with all of this. Due to the symptoms I have just described, my sleep is punctuated by periods of nervousness, making it impossible for me to recover my health with a good night's rest.

Please write back as soon as you can, Anne. Make your letter such that I can read it aloud to Charles and young Charles to inform them of how much you support my views in the matter of this ridiculous Harville attachment. Such disgrace it is bound to bring to the Elliot name. It makes me in need of my lavender water to soothe my temples.

Fondly,

Mary Musgrove

Mary, Mary, Mary... My heart was very gladdened to hear the news of young Charles and Claire making their engagement public. It seemed that he was willing to weather the storm of his mother's temper as long as his father and grandmother approved. I had no doubt that consideration of the Elliot name never entered into their opinions. I was the only Elliot relative that had made an effort to acquaint myself with young Charles Musgrove and his sisters and brothers, so I doubted the disapproval of Sir Walter Elliot and Miss Elizabeth Elliot, always at either Bath or the estate of Lady Dalrymple, was barely a consideration. My main concern was where the newly married couple might live that they would be the most out of the way of Mary's daily sour mood? Ah, well. Every couple in love encountered trials to be overcome. What her husband, poor Charles, would have to endure in the way of loud complaints! I was certain he would find he was much more needed in the running of the Uppercross fields in the near future.

While I leaned in my chair, contemplating how the housing of Uppercross must be in want of a shuffling so that Claire and Mary Musgrove would not share the same roof, the sound of a very cheery melody came to my ear. Intrigued, I stood and went to the door of my cabin. Very distinctly, I could make out a rough tune being played on a fiddle and fife. Then a very peculiar beating joined in, not unlike a drum, but much more hollow in sound.

My curiosity aroused, I opened the door and peered out. One of the very young ship's boys, Stanley, I thought, had a fife and was dancing out a barefoot jig as he played. Another older seaman was scratching away on a fiddle. Yet another had two belaying pins, typically used when securing the ropes of the running rigging lines from the sails to the bulwarks, to beat out a drum on the top of a mostly empty barrel, which caused the hollow thud of the sound. A ship of that size was too small for a drummer to be used to issue commands; therefore, I supposed the jury-rigged drum was the next best thing.

Captain Price, observing the men from a dignified distance, came to me with a smile.

"Aye, Mrs Wentworth, I hope you'll not use this moment to judge my abilities as a captain. There is not much for the men to do while we sit and wait. So I've let it be known that they are welcome to make merry for a bit each afternoon. There are only so many times we can scrub the deck with the holystone without them becoming anxious about the futility of it."

"Very wise, Captain Price. I understand special considerations must be made to keep the men happy during the idleness that a ship under the yellow jack flag may experience. We are fortunate that idleness is our main concern and not illness, excepting for Ross. You were wise to clean and fumigate so quickly once he became sick."

"I never could tolerate an unclean ship, Mrs Wentworth. I have been under captains who allowed some of the routines of orderliness and cleanliness to slide, and it was not good for the health or the morale of the ship."

"I never considered it from that perspective, sir. I suppose that in such close quarters, morale itself could suffer from a lack of hygiene."

We stood in silence a few minutes more, enjoying the music on that calm and pleasant day.

"Captain Price, I do not wish to presume, but back to your point of warding off ill tempers that arise from boredom, I think that my little square piano could be set up out here on pleasant days for a few songs. Also, I have a few books from Captain Wentworth. If you think any of the young boys would like to hear some stories, I would be happy to read aloud to them in the afternoons. I believe that he included *Rob Roy*, perhaps for that very reason. It is a tale of adventure that the younger seamen may enjoy."

"That is a capital idea, Mrs Wentworth. To hear someone with formal learning on an instrument will be a treat. And goodness knows some of the younger lads could do with more schooling. We are too small for a schoolmaster like the big ships have."

"Wonderful, if the weather holds out pleasantly, we could set it up tomorrow afternoon."

CHAPTER TWENTY-FOUR

That evening, I dined with Captain Price and his first lieutenant in my cabin. It was an unusually fine meal of fresh vegetables, fish, and fruits. I had noticed several of the seamen with their fishing poles out that afternoon in hopes of catching a fresh meal while we were stationed so. Some among them must have had a stroke of luck at it.

Captain Price informed me of his family back home in Portsmouth. His father had been a lieutenant in the navy, unable to advance further due to injury and, perhaps, lack of ability, though that was left unsaid. His mother hailed from a fine family, and his sister was married to a country parson, the second son of Sir Thomas Bertram. He spoke affectionately of his sister Fanny, and I gleaned that she was a person of high moral standards and intelligence whom he held very dear.

Much later, the night was still calm and soothing. I retreated to my berth and opened the first in the bundle of old letters from Frederick. The candlelight illuminated the interior of the ship's cabin most warmly and gave the effect of my being tucked away in a very cosy spot.

Dear Anne,

It has been some time since I have put pen to paper to write to you. I am in a state of complete exhaustion, but unable to make my mind rest long enough so that sleep can overcome me. I am worn from many hours of physical and mental labour, yet I am unable to settle myself. Perhaps that is the very reason my thoughts turn back to you. Broken down are the numerous distractions that keep me too busy for my heart and mind to find the opportunity to reflect on you, Anne. I have garnered the professional reputation over the years of being inexhaustible physically and mentally and always ready for action on the seas. Some of this is the nature of my character. But some of this is due to the fact that when I am consumed by my duties as a captain, there is very little spark left in me to brood over my ill-fated love for Miss Anne Elliot.

I have been awake for two full days now. Our ship is finally out of danger, and I have made myself come to my cabin and sit quietly. In this state of nerves and exhaustion, my mind can only be satisfied by unburdening myself to you.

It was almost three days ago that we entered the dreaded doldrums in the middle of the Atlantic between the Americas and the West Coast of Africa. Could I but describe in words the peculiar dread that enters the heart of every seaman, from the lowliest ship's boy to the most decorated admiral, when you see the wind die down completely from the sails. The tide disappears so that nothing in the water forwards the motion of the ship. A stillness not unlike the first few moments when you witness a soul leaving a body consumes the entire ship, from the deepest recesses of the hold to the top planks aloft in the crow's nest. It is as if God himself has decided to withdraw his presence and you are only left in stillness and silence. I would gladly take the strongest winds that I have ever encountered any day over that sickening stillness of absolutely no wind. 'No wind' hardly does it justice. No life would be a better term. Even the livestock on board become quiet, uneasy, and quarrelsome.

We had just escorted several Indiaman merchant ships to the island of St Helena for restocking before the treacherous trip around the southern tip of Africa. We had a brief shore leave and replenished our stores of water and food. Fresh ships were there to continue on with the merchant ships on their voyage to India. HMS *Laconia* was to return to England. And so we began under a fair wind to retrace our steps back north.

We had just passed Ascension Island and were out into open seas when we spotted a large French ship of the line in the distance behind us. I could get no clear view of her abilities, but I could very well see that she could outgun us easily. Out in the open waters with few tricks I could play on our pursuers, I decided to set full sail and outrun her.

'Do they expect to catch up to us, sir? It seems unlikely, as we have quite a lead on them. What can they be about?' Benwick queried from my side as we traded the spyglass back and forth to watch our pursuer.

'I don't like it, Benwick. They follow us as if they know something we don't.'

I determined we should take a more easterly tack, towards the African coast. If nothing else, we could try to ground their much larger ship in some shallow waters that we could navigate out of.

That is when the intent of the French ship became perfectly clear. In the short time we had been at port in St Helena, the doldrums had emerged along this latitude. There was virtually no wind and no tide. Our sails became limp and useless before our very eyes in a matter of minutes.

'They knew of these doldrums and chased us into them as if we were a fox before the hound!' I could not hide the bitterness from my voice. This unseen enemy had plotted with the French and surprised us by appearing after we had passed through a week before.

'But, won't they be as helpless as us, sir?' Benwick asked.

'No, by God, the size of their ship gives them access to winds higher up than our sails can reach! If there is any slight movement in the air, their ship will benefit first while we sit here like a sleeping duck in a pond!'

I looked again through my spyglass. The French ship seemed motionless with its sails hanging limp, but I knew it was just a matter of time before a slight puff brought them down on us. To put up a fight against a ship of that size, so outgunned, would be madness. Our advantage of speed and manoeuvrability would be gone. You can imagine my rage, Anne, at being left helpless and waiting. I paced the deck with a fury, despite the sun and stillness of the breeze. Finally, I decided, if we are to be captured, no one would accuse us of waiting quietly and accepting our fate without a fight.

I told a shocked Benwick to put in the boats and prepare the men for shifts of rowing.

'If we can't sail out of danger, perhaps we can pull *Laconia* out with rowing. It is the only chance we have. Divide the men into shifts, you and I included. But one of us is always on *Laconia*'s deck. And tell the men to be quick and quiet about it all. This manoeuvre may escape the notice of the French if we have luck. But noise and voices travel on still waters, so tell them to run silent about their business.'

So, now you know the source of my exhaustion, and why I turned to my writing to you on this weary evening.

We rowed, every man on the ship, in shifts, towing *Laconia* by towlines attached to our longboats. Through the day and the night, and the day and the night again. The ropes from our small boats reached up to *Laconia* and pulled her by sheer force through those deadly still waters. During my time back on deck, I could see that the French ship was disappearing in the distance. Even if they had boats in the water rowing to pursue us, the size of her would slow them down.

The mind does funny things when you are at the oar for so long, Anne. Your mind wanders as repetition without end and the muscles tire. There were times when I swear your voice called to me. Do you recall the very first piece of music I heard you play and sing to? That very first evening after I had instructed you as to the presence of maggots in the biscuits we eat on board a ship? I remember watching you sit at the instrument and wondering if my bold conversation had disgusted and insulted the most charming young woman I had ever laid eyes on. One never knows what is going on behind beautiful eyes. But, no, you looked up at me the moment your fingers struck that first chord. You looked directly in my eyes, and I saw the strong spirit in you. An arrow from the bow of Cupid could hardly have been more effective. The lyrics of that song you played floated back up and ran through my mind with each agonising pull of the oar. My back burnt, the sun beat upon me mercilessly, but I cared not. It was as sweet to me as the coolest drink of fresh water. It put iron back in my blood, and I rowed harder and encouraged those around me to do the same.

By the beginning of the third day, we all were stripped of our shirts and glazed over in sweat. I took my spyglass and looked at the very faint, distant French ship, languishing like a spot on the horizon. That is when our reprieve was delivered. The wind, shy at first, teased the top sails. All of us stopped and watched, holding our breath. The tease swelled itself into a full push of breeze. *Laconia* lurched forward like a foal on new legs. The shout that went up into the air, Anne, I swear they may have heard us back on the French ship. All the men jumped and laughed. I even smiled and laughed with them as I hurriedly put my shirt and jacket back on. We would be so far ahead of them, even if they caught the breeze soon, it would be a futile chase. I almost felt sorry for their captain, for it was a clever plan that almost worked, but my plan was even more clever. So we quickly outstripped the French ship as she made her way slowly out of the doldrums. The gloom that resides on a ship sitting in that smothering quiet quickly lifted.

I can feel now that my eyelids have grown heavier. Speaking to you has been a tonic for my weary spirit and limbs. Of my many close shaves as a captain, this one was one of the closest. Honestly, Anne, I had little hope of success, but the idea of sitting and waiting to be overtaken was something that rankled my spirit. I hope that the men drew strength from seeing their captain straining his back just as hard as they did. Perhaps those few extra hands at the oars were the difference between success and defeat. I wish I could inform them of the lovely young woman from Somersetshire to whom we owe our salvation. The memories of you lifted my spirit when all I wanted was to lay my head down and surrender.

Yours,
Captain Frederick Wentworth
HMS Laconia

I folded the letter and extinguished my candle. The warmth of the evening had dissipated slightly, and the sea outside lapped gently on the hull of the ship.

I went back to that evening in my mind, trying to recall the piece of music he referenced. But all I was able to summon from my recollections was the warmth I had felt on my cheeks, knowing that the handsome naval officer had his focus on me and me alone. There were other ladies there who may have been comelier, but it was for myself alone that his attention seemed fixed. What had started for me as an innocent enthusiasm to learn more of the true nature of life aboard ships had rapidly taken on a more passionate inclination. I recalled sitting at the piano, feeling warmer than I ever had in my life, and seeking out Frederick as my fingers struck the very first note. He could have been chatting or wandering the room, but instead his eyes were fixed upon me and lit from within by strong emotions that I could only guess at. What song I played or how well my voice lifted after that, I have no recollection. My entire mind and body had been wrapped in a cocoon of heat, and the sound of my heart in my ears was all I could discern. The memory increased the warmth of the evening as I drifted into sleep.

CHAPTER TWENTY-FIVE

The next morning was another fine day with more of a breeze blowing in from the sea. After a quick breakfast, I had some warm tea made for Midshipman Ross and took it below deck for him.

I found the doctor standing over him with his fingertips to his wrist.

"Is his pulse stronger today, doctor?"

"A little, I believe. It is well that only he went into that part of the city with its stagnant, low waters. Otherwise, it would be a ship full of dire cases."

I began to minister the tea to the still feverish and confused Ross. At one point, he claimed me to be his mother, and I did not disabuse him of the idea. I held his hand till I saw him in a somewhat restful sleep.

The doctor, feeling the need to rescue some of Ross's reputation, said, "Please, Mrs Wentworth, take no offence at anything he says while ill. He is not in his right mind."

"Mr Cole, please set yourself at ease. I have been at the side of many sick seamen over the years and even assisted with the injured after battles when my services could be of true help. I am familiar with the ramblings of a mind assaulted by fever or pain."

"That is good to hear. I was concerned as to how you may take what he is saying. He is a good lad, generally, and would be loath to give offence to any lady."

"I suppose after the next day or two, we will know more as to his fate."

"Yes, ma'am. The only good thing about yellow fever is that it strikes quickly and has done its work within about five days. Whether he lives or dies will be known by tomorrow morning, I think. And if he is the only one aboard to have developed symptoms, it is likely that we may be allowed on land sooner than a fortnight."

Later that morning, I spied the approach of a boat from the HMS *Stoic*. I could see Frederick as he caught sight of me. I wished terribly that I could have given a letter to him for Mary. But, while ones from shore could send us letters and supplies, anything coming from the ship to go back to shore was strictly prohibited.

After we greeted one another and he was assured that I was doing as well as could be expected, I asked Frederick to conduct some business that he would find distasteful indeed.

"Would you mind terribly, Captain Wentworth, to send a brief response to Mrs Mary Musgrove, telling her that she may have to wait longer than expected for a response from me. Let her know I am very well, but if you could explain the circumstances. She is expecting a reply that would contain some advice for her about a certain situation."

Frederick frowned, obviously not pleased with this particular charge. He glanced back at his men in the boat. "What situation would that be, Anne? Is it really that urgent?"

"Ahem, to do with her son and a certain situation that has

arisen of late." I certainly knew that I could say no more to a boat full of men who, even though they stared straight ahead in stony attention, were no doubt hanging on every single word for the benefit of the ship's gossip. "Just inform her of my state and that any reply will be delayed. Thank you."

I knew by how he bowed his head that this was the least appealing task that I could have demanded of him. Frederick preferred keeping interactions with my family to a minimum for reasons that I was very sympathetic to. If he could have begged off without the eyes and ears of his men behind him recording every word, he would have.

After I got a very reluctant consent, he threw up the rope and another small packet was sent up to me.

I returned to my cabin and unwrapped the oilcloth to investigate what Frederick had sent. Contained within were two letters and several fresh rolls that I recognised as being the work of Maude. While excelling in so many areas of the domestic arts, cooking was a skill over which Maude had little mastery. It was not from lack of effort to achieve mastery, but rather an inability to refine the subtleties of the art of cooking and, more especially, baking. With a wry grin, I wondered whether Frederick had included the dense little flour and water sculptures to add weight to the bundle so that it had more heft to toss up to our ship.

I opened the first letter that was in a sprawling, blocky hand.

Dear Mrs Wentworth,

We all wait eagerly for your return. I baked these rolls for you. I hope you feel well. Nelly and young Freddie are well. He made a friend of one of the local boys. His name is Moses. They run often in the greenery. Nelly made herself sick on mangoes. I don't give them to her for a while, but I see her spy a tree in the yard that has mangoes on it. She is a deep one at thinking. Freddie wants to say things to you. Come home soon.

Maude Smith

Mama,

Do not worry about me, I am having a grand time. Moses showed me all the fruit trees near our house. I helped Maude spell some of her words, just like you teached me. I do miss you. Nelly is loud at night for you, but the wet nurse helps calm her. Upon your return, please tell Nelly that we do not like her noise at night. Now that she walks, I am teaching her to climb. I am a proper big brother. I am making you proud. Come home soon.

Yours,

Frederick Elliot Wentworth

The combined letter of Freddie and Maude lifted my spirits considerably. I was grateful that everyone seemed to be finding their ways to cope with my absence so well.

I looked at the small pile of rolls that were sitting on the table. Perhaps if the ship's boys who fished during their leisure time needed some kind of bait for their hooks, the rolls would serve the purpose quite well. I was missing the cooking of Betsy still at home in England, maintaining our empty house for our eventual return. Her light touch with baked goods was one of the things that I was eager to experience again.

I picked up the next letter. It was from Lady Russell and had a small note from Frederick attached to the top.

Dear Anne,

We miss you terribly. This letter from Lady Russell was misplaced during the sorting of the mailbag. Return to us soon.

Yours,

Frederick

I immediately opened the newly found letter.

Dear Anne,

I hope your travels were uneventful as you made your way to the very distant shores of Barbados. I am well, and I had the very great pleasure of attending a card party at the residence of Sir Walter and your sister Elizabeth. It was a splendid evening with many of the elite of Bath society present.

I have received the alarming information from your sister Mary that her son Charles is engaged to a very questionable young lady from the Harville family. It gives me no pleasure to inform you that I think this an unwise match, Anne. I have the full support of your father and sisters in this opinion and eagerly await word from you.

I understand that you had a brief acquaintance with this young lady, and I wish to know more of her. Any intelligence you may be able to convey would be appreciated. It would be a great misfortune to have the grandson of Sir Walter Elliot attached in this manner to the daughter of a penniless sailor. I expect little disagreement from the Musgroves, since this union does them no honour. All of the honour is given by the Musgroves who will receive no title in return and little, if any, wealth. It is a most concerning development.

You should be aware that, by association, this marriage would do little to further the future prospects of Freddie and Nelly Anne to make matches of advantage. Relations of this sort can do nothing to build back the wealth of the Elliots. I eagerly await your response so that I may further enlighten Charles Musgrove and his son to the proper objections that the rest of the family have in response to this development.

Cordially yours,

Lady Russell

Even halfway round the world, quarantined in a frigate out on the water, I was still not safe from the outrages and intrigues at which my family and friend were so adept. I sighed and stood to pace the very confined area of my cabin. To imagine that, of all people, I would stand as an impediment in the path towards happiness of these two very worthy young people. How could my own people know me so little? And by what right did Lady Russell drag the names of my children into the business? And Captain Harville, whom I had witnessed in action for England, who lives in discomfort from injuries received during service, who came to aid Frederick on multiple occasions of extreme danger during battle, to be dismissed as a penniless sailor?

It vexed me so that I had to abandon the oppressive cabin altogether and take several turns about the deck to create a wind with which to cool my cheeks. I prayed that I would be a parent who was familiar enough with the temperaments of my children that I could support them in their decisions and raise objections solely for their future happiness and safety. I found the pleas for me to exert my influence on those who loved me to be infuriating, especially when my own history was considered. Claire and young Charles were very suited to each other, as anyone who had bothered to place considerations such as temperament and disposition into account would know.

I was thankful that my current situation made it an impossibility to write back. It would give my temper time to cool before I put pen to paper. Responses to Mary and Lady Russell would take time and thought to answer with calm consideration. However unlikely, I secretly hoped that Claire and young Charles would elope and have done with all the conflict.

Captain Price, seeing me making rounds about the deck, offered to retrieve my piano. "One of the officers informed me that the boatswain was complaining of an aching knee. The men take it as a sure sign that there may be rain approaching, although I see no cloud in the sky. You would do the *Lucille* and her crew a great honour with your music, Mrs Wentworth."

"It would be my pleasure, Captain. But only if the ship's boy, Stanley, I think? Yes, only if Stanley promises to accompany me."

"I should hardly think you could stop him, ma'am! He has been terribly curious about your cargo that you have stowed away in the cabin. In fact, I am surprised that he has not knocked upon your door to request to see the thing. He can be a very determined young man."

The piano was brought to the deck and set atop two small barrels, and I sat before it with the most interested audience that I could ever have claimed to perform before. The youngest among the crew sat and stared with rapt attention. The older men were milling around, pretending their best to be busy at work in the general vicinity. I supposed all of them were exceedingly curious as to the nature of this boxy thing that had brought a captain's wife aboard their ship.

I struck out with a cheerful Scottish folk song that had a lovely rhythm to it. Because it had been quite some time since I had been at the keys of a piano, I thought the jaunty piece would very kindly hide any mistakes my indolent fingers might make. Then I moved into several pieces by Bach that were more meditative and solemn.

As I played a lovely little jig, I caught the eye of young Stanley and nodded for him to join in. He slowly stood and took his fife from his back pocket. He started to play, bashful at first, then with more gusto as the song took hold of him. By the end, he was stepping high to the song. A hearty round of applause greeted us upon our completion. Stanley looked at me through the mop of his mouse brown hair with a wide grin.

"Stanley, that was wonderful! How about one more? Do you have a favourite?"

He only nodded before putting his wooden fife to his mouth and beginning a familiar Irish folk song. I joined in, but allowed Stanley to continue to lead the melody while I supported him. Watching his confidence grow as he accompanied what to him must be a very fine instrument indeed was very gratifying. After several more songs, I had to leave off, as my fingers, unused to the work, began to ache.

"Stanley, that was really very good! You have some talent, I see."

"Thank you, Mrs Wentworth. It's an honour to accompany the likes of you. I never heard such music before."

"There are those who possess more talent than I, Stanley, but I do endeavour to improve myself through practise as much as I am able."

"Yes, ma'am. I try to practise as well."

"Where are you from?"

"London," Stanley muttered, shuffling his feet as the conversation steered from what was evidently one of his favourite topics.

"And your family? Do they live in London as well?"

"No, ma'am. I am from the Marine Society."

"Ah. I see." The Marine Society, begun almost one hundred years earlier, helped orphan boys escape from the streets of London and receive training for placement onto naval ships. Even though the dangers of a naval life were very real, three meals a day and a mostly dry place to sleep every night were a great appeal when compared to the hardships of London orphans.

"Captain Wentworth, my husband," I ventured to tell him, "has informed me multiple times that the war against Napoleon would never have been won if not for the brave young men of the Marine Society. He has frequently remarked that the bravest and best seamen had their start that way and did quite well for themselves over time. Thank you so much for your service, Stanley."

I extended my hand to him. He looked up at me with

surprise on every feature of his nut-brown face. Quickly, he rubbed his hand on the side of his britches in an effort to clean it, then extended it out as one might approach a large dog of uncertain temperament. We shook hands. The surprise turned into a broad, lopsided grin on Stanley's face before he withdrew his hand hastily.

"Stanley, I am missing my children terribly. It always soothes me to read to them. Would you be so kind as to allow me to read to you and the other boys for a few minutes?"

And that was how the rest of the afternoon was spent, in the pleasant company of the ship's boys. They looked up at me, rapt in their attention, as I read the tale of *Rob Roy*.

"Would anyone like a chance to read aloud?" I asked when my throat was worn with use. I was gratified to see Stanley's hand shoot up. I placed the book in his dirty hands and passed several enjoyable minutes listening to him let loose the words of adventure onto the winds and waves.

CHAPTER TWENTY-SIX

Later that evening, I was quite done in from the musical and literary appreciation society meeting on the deck. I realised that I had not yet read another of Frederick's letters from so many years ago. It must have been at least twelve years since he had written the last collection of correspondences. Settling in for the evening, I took one from the bundle and opened it.

Dear Anne,

The last week has seen me peeking around corners and scanning the streets. I am in London, visiting Sophy and Admiral Croft. They are in drydock here while the admiral strategises with the Admiralty as to the best ways to continue and strengthen the blockades of the French coastal cities.

My good luck has been that blockading those coastal cities from sending or receiving supplies has never been assigned to me. To always be sitting and watching and waiting, I would go mad. A captain far from England can be his own man to some extent and not always be under the watchful gaze of the Admiralty. But so close to England as the French coast, it is a place where you must always be wary of the judgment of your superiors. The freedom of the East or West Indies, even the Mediterranean is more desirable than blockading the French coast. I hope that I am posted to an area of the world where I have previously enjoyed much freedom in my command decisions.

London used to be very amusing when I was on leave, but not any longer. I can never be easy here just as I can never be easy in Bath. I can never again be calm if I were to go into the county of Somersetshire. I know you travel but little from Kellynch Hall, yet the feeling that I may by accident encounter you in one of those places torments me.

It is unlikely that we should meet anywhere unless I intentionally seek you out. But every time I wander into the stall of a bookseller, or attend a performance of a piece of music that I know would be of interest to you, I am on high alert for a glimpse of your profile. Every woman who bears the slightest resemblance to you in face or figure starts my heart up like a hare startled from the hedgerow. Perhaps, one day, if I wed someone whom I esteem, I will no longer suffer from this anxiety. There is no shortage of pretty young women here. Perhaps this will be the time; maybe I will find another—

I know that these letters will never be read by you, so I have no scruples to write of the true scare that I did have at a musical performance the other night. It was a lovely Mozart concert that I was enjoying very much. I looked off to the side and noticed a profile that struck deep at my core, Anne.

It was Lady Russell. And she met my gaze and held it. Her face was unreadable, as always. It took some mighty effort on my part to turn my focus back to the musicians.

Planning to leave at the intermission, I was making for the door when Lady Russell stepped in front of me. I had intended to pass her with no more than a curt greeting, but she guided me to an alcove to speak in private. I would be lying if I said that I had no curiosity as to what she was going to say.

'Lady Russell, we have no reason to revisit any former acquaintance that we enjoyed. Unless you have something of importance to say...'

'Do you not wish to know of Miss Anne Elliot, Captain Wentworth?'

Trapped, I stared at her. She was an unreadable enemy ship with a stratagem that I could not discern. Anger rose in me. But I stood still, waiting. I would in no way beg her for information.

'Are you not the least bit curious as to how my young friend Anne is faring? You two were quite close not so very many years ago, were you not, Captain Wentworth?'

'It is of little importance to me, Lady Russell. Please feel no obligation to enlighten me as to the latest news from Somersetshire. We were well acquainted enough for you to know I take little pleasure in idle talk.'

'So that is where Anne stands in your estimation, Captain. As a topic of idle conversation? No more than a shadow of a memory? Well, we were a little acquainted, were we not? I have noticed your professional progress in the newspapers. You have done very well for yourself and lived up to everyone's expectations.'

'I have been very fortunate in my postings and the men assigned to my ships. I like to think that while some of my success is due to my capacity as a captain, more is due to the natural talents of my men.'

'I suspect the majority of your progress can be accredited solely to your ability to command. You are frequently mentioned in the papers as being exceptionally brave and clever. The many battles you have helped win and the enemy ships you have captured. Yes, you look very capable. Very capable indeed.'

Something in the tone of her voice caused my spine to stiffen, Anne. Or perhaps it was the tilt of her head, or the way the candlelight cast shadows on her face. I could not make out what this was about. There were few ways she could injure me more than she had already done in the past. The only possible way for her to cause me more injury was if she took my sword and ran me through.

With a toss of her head and a laugh, she continued, 'I must say, you surprise me. I imagined that if I ever saw you again you would be on your knees begging me for information of Miss Anne Elliot. I was utterly mistaken, I see. The years have cured you of that brief infatuation. You must truly be recovered from your little attachment to her. Perhaps it was not so very enduring after all.'

'Please do not presume to imagine that you know anything of my feelings, Lady Russell.'

I bowed and turned to leave, but she placed a hand on my forearm, detaining me with the slightest pressure.

'If you find, sir, that you are to be staying in town

for much longer and wish to call on me, here is my card.'

She drew a card from the inside of her glove and handed it to me. I looked down at it, puzzled. It was her calling card with her address.

'I do not—'

'Captain Wentworth. Since you no longer have feelings for my friend, and you will be in London for a while, perhaps you could call on me to discuss music, or any other topic that you wish.' She placed her hand on my arm again. 'I am happy to oblige a brave navy officer such as yourself by providing some—diversions, shall we say?'

I recoiled from her touch.

She stepped closer and whispered, 'Think about it, Frederick. I imagine you must be lonely, pining after a mere child for so many years. I was a married woman, after all, and not so very much older than you. I know what I am about. My husband has been many years gone from this world and, on rare occasions, I miss the company of a gentleman.'

I stumbled back, into another patron. Barely mustering an apology, I turned and left the theatre. Indescribable fury fuelled my insensible wandering through the streets of London that night. My head spun mercilessly. Had someone approached me with ill intent, I would have beaten them to a pulp, the red was so thick before my eyes. No amount of walking slacked it.

To imagine that we had solicited Lady Russell's aid in our attempt to gain your father's approval for our marriage. And now, when she believes I no longer feel anything for you... Does this mean she is assured that you no longer have feelings for me? Does this mean you are happily married to another?

I must take this to mean that there is truly no hope, Anne. If you were still in love with me, surely your closest friend would not make such a proposition? Did her refusal to advocate for our union arise from a duplicity of intentions? I am so confused and have no one to unburden myself to.

The sooner I am out at sea, the better. I hope for a posting that requires decisive action. In the face of danger is the only time when my heart feels free of all remembrance of you. Sometimes I wish to God that fateful evening when you enquired about my banging a biscuit on the side of a plate had never occurred. I would be a whole man walking this world instead of the shell I sometimes feel myself to be. Would that we could have a few moments of conversation together; perhaps that would ease my suffering. If I could but correspond with you! But here, all courage flees. I could not survive another break from you. I would be utterly undone. I would not survive it. I can never risk attempting to gain your hand again. It is done.

Yours,

Captain Frederick Wentworth

There was a blast of light from the starboard side of the ship. The rolling of thunder that followed rattled the timbers from bow to stern. A stiff wind blew and caused the planks beneath me to roil as the *Lucille* was buffeted by the rising wind. I raised my eyes from the letter and stared, unseeing, at the light from my lantern.

My mind raced, trying with little success to push past a tangled bramble of pain and confusion to the truth. Lady Russell and I had had so few conversations relating to Frederick after the engagement was broken. The times I did raise his name, she would change the subject and continue on as if she had not heard. It had been such a trial for me to discuss Frederick without tears filling my eyes that I had rarely spoken of him. I soon learnt to never say his name and try to interest myself in the lives of those around me without reflecting on the regret that weighed me down. With a flush of anguish, I recalled a conversation with Frederick after he had gone to my father to seek his blessing of our marriage.

'Your father did not approve or disapprove of our engagement, Anne. But the chill in his tone cannot be mistaken for joy,' Frederick had said with downcast eyes.

'You are unaccustomed to the manner of my father. I am sure that I can sway him to view our marriage in a more pleasing light.'

'Anne, I begin to think that Sir Walter, a baronet, will never welcome the marriage of his middle daughter to a newly made captain of the Royal Navy. Would that I had saved a little more of the prize money I had made as a first lieutenant, this may have been avoided. But before I met you, I had no reason to plan for the future. I was a foolish young man. I spent money freely because I had no beacon to guide my heart to better choices. Not like I do now.'

I placed my palm to his cheek in an effort to chase away any recrimination.

'You were a very unaffected young man who had funds for

the first time in his life and was eager to enjoy himself. Few could find it in their hearts to admonish you. I know I certainly cannot.'

I could see that my words were not lifting Frederick's spirits. A new thought entered my mind.

'My father will occasionally allow himself to be guided by the wisdom of my friend, Lady Russell. Indeed, she is in many ways a member of our family. Perhaps, if we were to inform her of our engagement and ask her to attempt to influence my father?'

My heart tore in two, recalling how Frederick's eyes had lit up at this sliver of hope.

'Yes! Lady Russell! She may be able to sway him with her sense and interest in your happiness. Though I think that perhaps she does not hold me in high esteem. Sometimes she looks at me in such a severe way, I am not sure that she would approve of our engagement.'

'All will turn out well, love,' I said as I gave Frederick a quick, bashful kiss on the cheek.

But the wind of Lady Russell's interference had blown in the opposite direction. Her advice to my father was to oppose our marriage with even more forcefulness. To reject any aid or support, and to withhold any sanction of our union. And then, to discover that she had solicited Frederick's company when she knew how I languished in low spirits for years afterwards—was there any excuse that could clear her character in this?

If I could go back, if I could just return to that moment

when I advised we seek out the patronage of Lady Russell, I would have done the complete opposite and suggested an elopement. I should have told Frederick to find a carriage and take me to Gretna Green that very night. Although Frederick was a man of honour to his core, he would have done it if I had persisted, if I had persuaded him with words and kisses.

I tore my eyes from the glow of the lantern and saw another, closer flash of lightning. The thunder rattled my bones, and I felt suddenly hollow. Where were my rage and indignation? I should have been furious, but all I felt was sorrow at her misguided concern and her...her loneliness? Why else would she actively pursue Frederick in such an improper way?

Another clap of sound and light, closer than anything I had ever experienced, burst upon me. Storms grazed the earth so much more closely in this part of the world. I heard footsteps on deck as measures were being taken to prepare the frigate. I hoped that none of the men would be struck by a bolt of lightning, which sometimes occurred on ships.

I gazed back down at the letter in my hand. The fact that Frederick had made a real effort to befriend Lady Russell after our marriage, the fact that he could even tolerate being in the same room with her, spoke so deeply of his intent to start anew with my family and friends when we finally did wed. Not for the first time, I realised that even though my family and friend had claim to the nobler lineage, we did not have claim to a nobler spirit than was to be found in the breast of Frederick Wentworth. Never in our marriage of ten years had he mentioned this incident. To disparage Lady Russell for a hurtful occurrence from so long ago would be beneath him. He had obviously forgiven Lady Russell; I must try to do the same.

I curled into my bunk, expecting sleep would be a late

visitor that night. I forced my eyes shut as the lightning flashed in the same manner that memories forced their way across the landscape of my mind. The sea rolled under me as the gathering storm blew the scent of sharp lightning and sweet rain into the small cabin.

CHAPTER TWENTY-SEVEN

S omehow, despite the raging storm outside, my mind
calmed enough to fall into a fitful sleep. I had experienced enough terrible weather on ships to be somewhat familiar with the sensation. I was one who rarely
experienced seasickness. More than the storm, the contents
of Frederick's letter swirled through my imagination,
making sleep a skittish prospect.

In what must have been the morning, a drizzle of wet
upon my face awakened me. It was raining heavily outside in
nonstop sheets. Sloops and frigates such as the HMS *Lucille*
were frequently refitted prize ships captured from other
countries and not as watertight as those that were English
built. Another splash on my cheek made me sit up in fright
as I glanced to the table that contained my letters. Through
the very dim light, I perceived that the surface appeared dry.

I got out of bed and snatched up the precious correspondences. A crack of lightning and thunder in the distance told
me of yet another approaching storm. I placed the letters
under my pillow.

The wind was picking up dramatically, and a sudden lurch of the ship beneath me caused me to stumble and fall to the ground. I heard the rapid steps of men and shouting from the deck. I dressed as well as I could while the ship rolled and pitched. As I approached the door, I was thrown against it suddenly and took a sharp blow to my shoulder.

Undeterred, I braced myself and pried the door open. The ship then thrust me out of the cabin, and my stomach went square into the railing near the wheel of the ship. The quartermaster on duty did not take his steely eyes from the water in front of him or remove his hands from the wheel to offer assistance.

"Mornin', Mrs Wentworth," he said, cool as can be. "A bit of a brisk day. If you don't mind my saying, I expect Captain Price would rather you keep to the cabin."

I looked out into the sky. It was the angriest set of dark, low-flying clouds that I had ever seen. What looked to be debris from onshore, leaves and small branches, flew past us even though we were far from land. The quartermaster strained against the wheel with all his might, muscles bulging and knuckles white. The deck of the ship swung about like a child's toy in the bath, making the world around us spin and bob dramatically.

"Why do we fly around like this?" I cried.

"The anchor cable snapped, ma'am. We have no anchor. In this wind and with another arm of the storm blowing in, well…"

He suddenly began spinning the wheel in the other direction, gripping tightly again. I could see that he was trying with all the strength in his arms to steady the direction of the ship and keep us away from shore. It was an almost impossible task to accomplish with just the rudder, and I knew well enough that a lady chattering in his ear was unhelpful. Someone bodily crashed into me from behind. Gripping the rail, I swung around to set eyes on the tired face of Captain Price.

"My apologies, ma'am," he shouted over the wind that had risen to such a pitch as to make conversation almost an impossibility. "I suggest you return to your cabin for now."

Through a combination of stumbles and falls, I squeezed myself back into the cabin. I fell to the floor as the ship lifted and attempted to throw me in the rest of the way. A slosh of salty water followed me and wetted my dress. I crawled to the door and shoved it closed with my feet, collapsed to my back, and panted for a few moments.

As I lay there on the wet wood of the cabin floor, through the roar of the wind, I heard the capstan bars being slid into place and the men turning the capstan by pushing it around in a circle. Usually this would be terribly hard work, as they would be bringing up an anchor. But, unfortunately, the wild winds and the shifting of the ship in the middle of the night meant that the anchor of the *Lucille* was somewhere at the bottom of the bay and not on the anchor cable. The men were hauling in a relatively light cable with no anchor in order to avoid it getting irretrievably caught on the seafloor. Should the cable get caught and suddenly go taut as the ship was blown strongly, I imagined it could tear a hole straight through the hull and be the end of us.

All in all, I was beginning to think that flat on my back on the floor was one of the wisest positions I could be in. I had settled into it for a moment when the chair next to me decided to make a flying go at my face. I covered my head with my forearms just before it would have crashed down on me. Reluctantly, I squirmed towards my berth and crawled up into it.

My clothing clung with an uncomfortable, warm dampness, but when I heard the shouts and cries of the men on deck attempting to bring some semblance of order while getting constantly knocked about, I had no reason to complain. I said a silent prayer for the men to keep their feet firmly on deck and not to get swept away over the railings and into the sea. I prayed for Frederick to be safe in his ship. I prayed for my children to be safe and comforted with Maude whom they both looked on as a second mother. I prayed that Captain Price and Sara Price would live to see each other again.

I reached my hand under the berth to touch the smooth wood of the square piano that was lashed down tightly. I smiled. The smile turned into a laugh as tears rolled down my cheeks. For want of music. That was why I was being flung about by the angry sea on a plague ship far from those I loved. Humour sometimes sprang upon me in moments of distress.

When my laugh waned, I tried to think of any service I could provide in the present situation. My years as a captain's wife had taught me that when a ship was well run with a highly trained crew being directed by a man of ability, sometimes the best service one could render was keeping well out of the way. If I had a way of safely going below deck, I could offer solace to Midshipman Ross. To rise and exit the cabin again, a formidable task in itself, then to traverse the short way to the hatch and climb down the ladder with the fury of this endless storm swirling around could prove deadly. With any luck, Ross had survived the night and broken his fever. What an awful circumstance in which to be dreadfully ill. It was terrifying enough when one was in perfect health.

A wild swing grabbed hold of the ship, and the angry chair spun on its side and skittered to the other side of the room. I glanced about. Nothing, other than the rogue chair, was in danger of loosening and flying around the small space. Everything was generally made to be secure for an occurrence such as this.

With little else to do and fearing for their safety, I reached under my pillow and retrieved the stack of letters. The letters from Mary and Lady Russell were put to the side. The other letters from Frederick, including the brief note from him when I had left on this journey, were refolded and organised. I held out the unopened ones and placed the others in an oilcloth and tied them tight. If need be, I would place them in my bodice so nothing happened to them.

After that bit of organising, I sat and waited. The ship was still swinging wildly, the men still shouted from the decks and below. Water found its way through the most minor slivers in the cabin walls to occasionally spray me. Finally, to distract my busy mind, I opened one of the unread letters from Frederick. Despite the pitching and rolling of the wooden world around me, this slip of paper unfolding before me gave me hope and strength beyond measure.

Dear Anne,

Something quite unusual has occurred that makes me wonder if my mind is seeing connexions where none exist. We are back in the West Indies and had just captured a pirate ship. I was at my desk, making entries into the ship's log of the day's activities, when Benwick burst in.

'Sir, one of the prisoners...' Benwick seemed most discomfited; I had no idea as to the cause.

'He—I mean... He, sir. Is not.'

'Are you drunk, Benwick?'

'No! Sir. We were stripping and washing the prisoners, one was being particularly feisty, and well, he is a woman, sir.'

'Damn your eyes, Benwick, if this is a jest. As you can see, I'm in no mood.'

He paled, noticeably. 'It is not a jest, I swear. Should I bring the prisoner to you?'

Despite my fatigue, I was certainly curious and nodded warily.

Benwick shortly returned with the prisoner. Anne, you could have bowled me over with a feather. Now that some of the grime had been washed away, a very handsome, tall, sturdy woman stood before me in the grubby garments of a pirate. Her close-cropped hair, an unremarkable brown, was plastered down upon her head from the forced bath they were all receiving. Her prominent chin, heavy brows, and the grim set of her mouth was more of what one would see on a man. Those proud eyes were sharp and glinted like steel. A tattoo of mermaids and hearts tangled up her fore-arms. I have encountered much to strike awe in any man during my time at sea, but this left me speechless for a moment.

'You are a woman?'

'So says your man here, if he has enough experience to know the difference.'

I could not help but smirk for just a second, Benwick was so profoundly nonplussed.

'And were you held against your will by those buccaneers?'

'As if they could keep me prisoner and live to tell the tale.'

I leant back in my chair and studied this puzzle before me. 'Your accent is American, I believe?'

'If that is how you hear me, so it may be.'

'You seem to have a bit of education about you.'

She remained silent. My mind worked furiously; a

memory was floating just out of reach. A portrait I had seen. Something I had read recently.

'What is your name?' I asked.

'Jade Dosa.'

'And that is your true name, given to you at birth?'

'It is what I answer to.'

'Miss Dosa, you realise the penalty for piracy will be hanging by the neck until—'

'I'm with child!' Her hand shot to cover her belly.

I sighed. 'I am no doctor and doubt if ours would be able to verify such a claim, so I will leave that to the courts to consider as they pass their final judgment on you. Benwick, if you would be so good as to clear out your cabin of your belongings and allow our guest, Miss Dosa, to remain there under the supervision of two marines at all times. See that she has good meals. If anything comes to me of behaviour unbecoming of any member of our crew towards her, they will receive a flogging around the fleet on our next visit to a harbour, understood?'

'Yes, sir.'

As they turned to leave, the fog lifted from my brain and the final lettered tile fell into place. A name, a face.

'Theodosia?'

Jade Dosa turned halfway before stopping and holding stiffly.

'I do not know who you speak of.' She spoke barely above a whisper.

'Hmm, my mistake. I do apologise, madam. Please forgive me. Is there anyone you wish me to contact for you? On a mainland somewhere? Perhaps in America? In the state of South Carolina?'

'Absolutely not. No one bothered to search for me

when I was lost, so why would I want them to find me now?'

'Fair point, Miss Dosa. Enjoy your stay and feel free to send me a message should you have need of anything.'

She had a good, harsh laugh at this. 'You have nothing I want.'

And with that, she left. I did not see her again until several days later when she and the rest of the prisoners were escorted off the ship. I informed the local authorities of her expected confinement that would disqualify her from hanging. I expect that she will not be held long by them if she is nearly as clever as I suspect.

I only confide in these sheets of paper, Anne, that I strongly suspect the woman, Jade Dosa, to have been Theodosia Burr Alston, the daughter of the former vice president of the United States, Aaron Burr, and the wife of the governor of South Carolina, Joseph Alston. I was given old newspapers from America and had read of the tale with some interest. *The Patriot*, the schooner Mrs Alston was travelling on, was sailing north to New York and is rumoured to have been found abandoned and run aground on the Outer Banks of North Carolina. It was assumed all aboard had been slaughtered by pirates. But I believe I encountered her, and for reasons that are solely her own, she wishes to remain unknown. Through some means, I believe the pirates were persuaded to spare her life, and she joined them. I have heard of lady pirates before, but never expected to encounter one.

Anne, moments like these, when I have such intriguing puzzles to unravel such as that of Jade Dosa, I wish every one of these letters could be held by you. I wish with all my heart that I could eagerly await a return letter from you. You would have some clever insight or additional fact to help me understand. I would press that sheet from your elegant hand to my chest and hope to catch some scent from it. But my hands remain empty after the delivery of every mailbag from England to our ship. The palms of my hands itch as if they can sense the missing puzzle piece of your correspondence that ought to be there. It is not to be, though. I have no one to confide in about this and many more things besides. A tale such as the one about the probable identity of our recent prisoner will not be entered into the ship's log, as it is mere specula-tion on my part. She will simply be entered into the ship's log as female pirate Jade Dosa, true identity unknown. Cutthroat she may be, but she is also a lady who wishes to continue to be unfound by her relatives and husband. I will respect her wishes. It seems that the secret of the former vice president's daughter will remain for me alone and these sheets of paper.

Once back to port, word reached me that Jade Dosa had been able to convince her guards to aid in her escape. She has disappeared. Perhaps our paths will cross again someday.

Yours,

Captain Frederick Wentworth

HMS Laconia

Frederick had not shared his suspicions as to the true identity of Jade Dosa with the world. It was so like him to admire the bravery of someone for forging their own path, just as he had done. The letter made me once again reflect on my own decisions to yield to the persuasions of others that went contrary to the instincts of my heart and the better judgment of my mind. Perhaps Theodosia had yielded to the influence of others her entire life and only had loneliness and unhappiness to show as her reward for her obedience. And when tragedy struck in the form of a pirate attack on the *Patriot*, an opportunity presented itself to let the world believe she was dead. A chance to start anew with a life of adventure. She grasped it and never looked back.

In some ways, I admired Theodosia. She saw her chance for fulfilment and freedom and took it. There was no need for her to brood over lost opportunities for years, as I did. They took a toll on one's spirit, years of contemplative study of the paths that one regretted not taking.

The ship heaved around me, and out of desperation to calm my rising unease, I grasped a second letter.

Dear Anne,

Another of my fine ruses has saved the day. It would irritate you to no end, I am sure, to hear of how frequently I find myself employing such methods. In a way, I find them more challenging and amusing than all of the bold actions I take during battle. When the alternative is capture or death, one uses every possible scheme at one's disposal, including dissembling and obfuscation. I rarely look back on any of these decisions with anything like regret.

We were on a cruise back from the Mediterranean. Orders had come in for our ship to make the return voyage so that we may add to the blockade of France. It is not an assignment that inspires, but necessary to keep the French fleet weak and scattered. Who knows how many times England would have been overrun with Napoleon's troops if it were not for these tedious blockades of ours keeping the French ships on a short leash?

We were a day out from reaching the Strait of Gibraltar and making our way back to England. The weather had forced us to hug the northern coast of Africa closer than I would wish. A sudden gale had split the mizzen topsail and blown away our main top gallant sail. While we were repairing these damages, a French privateer came into view.

I knew they were on the lookout for us because of the several merchant ships that we had captured in the area. We had garnered quite a reputation for being a thorn in the side of French activities in these waters. The ship outgunned us many times over and was coming up fast. Usually, we could have outmanoeuvred her and taken another prize, but our sails were compromised, so it would have been a one-sided duel of the *Laconia* being pounded by broadside after broadside from the French ship's cannons.

I hastily ordered that our colours should be struck. Once the Union Jack had been lowered and stowed away, I ordered the yellow jack, or quarantine flag, to be raised. All the officers removed their jackets and hats, and I instructed several of them to lounge on deck, near cannons of course in case things went awry, and smudge under their eyes with spent gunpowder from the firing mechanisms of the guns.

I then instructed Benwick to come to the railing and act as captain. Once the frigate was within range, its captain yelled at us in French through a speaking trumpet. Benwick responded in Dutch, a language he had been working to learn of late from one of the seamen. There was a confused exchange, and the only words that could be familiar in the babble were 'Quarantaine', 'Algiers', 'Plaag', and 'Pesten'. Thank God for Benwick's curiosity for new languages.

The French privateers raised their hands, motioning us away, and began to move off. We waited until they were well out of sight, allowing the ship to drift listlessly for at least an hour in case they were observing us through their spyglass, which is exactly what I would have done. It worked. Such deceptions can mean the difference between life and death.

Perhaps this will always be a point in which we cannot see eye to eye, but as a captain with the charge of so many souls on my ship, I will employ as many tactics for success as I can justify. After the sails were mended, we were on our way again.

We came into port at Portsmouth and had some free time while *Laconia* was receiving a new sheathing of copper for her hull. I received a plea from my good friend Captain Harville to sail his wife, sister, and cousin to Plymouth once we were back on the water, as that was our next stop before we were to report to the blockade.

Anne, those few days gave me a glimpse of hope for my heart and soul. Benwick and I dined with Mrs Harville and Fanny Harville several times before *Laconia* was cleared for sailing. In Fanny Harville's turn of mind, expressions, and a look in her eye when hearing something humorous, she reminded me very much of you, Anne. She is well-read, handsome, and likes nothing more than to get the dour Benwick to laugh at some clever observation of hers. If Benwick were not here, I was in a very fair way of developing some sort of regard for her. But next to the younger, dashing, serious, very well-read Benwick, I must appear as a bit of an old man with not as quick a mind. I am very happy for my first lieutenant. A more worthy man could not be found anywhere in all the ships of the navy, I believe. It is only a matter of time before he is made a master and commander of some sloop or frigate. Then I shall have to train up some new young man to the ways of running a ship.

In some ways, it is very difficult to see their young love blossoming, first on shore and now as we sail them to Plymouth to join Captain Harville. I take on as many duties as possible so that Benwick has more time to stroll the decks with Fanny Harville. Mrs Harville and I have exchanged many knowing looks over them. To have the pleasure of celebration, to know that they will only be met with joy and smiles when they announce their engagement, I feel a bit jealous, Anne.

Benwick will perhaps need a talking-to in order to strengthen his resolve before the window to propose to Miss Fanny Harville closes. That he thinks too little of himself is the only fault I could accuse him of. I recall so clearly every detail of the moment I proposed to you, Anne. It was born of the impulse of the moment after touching your hand that night. My overflowing heart had formed the words before my mind could consider.

That is the difference between Benwick and myself. He sometimes lets his mind talk his spirit out of a course of action. A woman such as Fanny Harville is rare, and no time or obstacle should be tolerated when you have your heart set upon her. He should propose and marry her as soon as may be so that no impediment blocks their way to happiness. I am glad for him. It has given me a lift in my spirits to know that perhaps another woman exists who can compare to Fanny Harville or even Anne Elliot.

I begin to think there is none who can replace an Anne Elliot, but perhaps almost be her equal. Next time I am turned out to shore for a good stretch of weeks, I am resolved to have a serious look about me and keep my weather eye open for one such as you or Fanny Harville. I wish to be like Captain Harville, eager for a chance at port to visit with my loved ones. Although his money does not match mine, I see the domestic riches he enjoys each time he encounters his wife. Seeing Fanny Harville and Mrs Harville has caused my mind, when I allow it to be reflective, to conjure images of Anne Elliot standing on a dock as my ship sails into port. I can almost feel your hand in mine as I help pull you up from the ladder when a longboat rows you out to greet me.

This is why inactivity is such a dangerous curse for me. I hope our turn at the blockades is not long, as the boredom of it will cause my mind to play scenes that will depress my spirits. Perhaps you are not plagued by such imaginings. I pray that you are not, Anne.

Yours,

Captain Frederick Wentworth

HMS Laconia

CHAPTER TWENTY-EIGHT

Oh, how I was indeed plagued by imaginings of what ought to have been. Frederick and I had been so protective of our precious time together since our marriage that we had rarely spoken of or reflected on those bleak years. Eight years lost forever.

I remembered so clearly what Frederick had said to me as we held hands under the churchyard's yew tree after our wedding ceremony—days before he had been summoned back to service due to Napoleon escaping from Elba.

'Let us not speak upon those terrible years, Anne. I want only to create pleasing, fond memories to outshine those dark times. I have seen how precious life is. I have had men standing next to me turned into a bloody mist by a cannon-ball or swept under by illness in no more than a day. The violence and diseases on ships carry men away like clouds on a windy day. We shall let the past keep itself company. We shall only live and talk of the present and future. Do you agree?'

Closing my eyes, I could remember the pain and sorrow that haunted his gaze as he made this request of me. What could I do but agree with a nod and long kiss? I was so grateful I did, for he had been called back into service just a week later. We had spent our days laughing and travelling the seaside, creating new, happy reflections for the lonely hours that were soon to come.

I opened my eyes again and saw the black pitching and spinning clouds above through the skylight of the cabin roof. Although I rarely ever experienced discomfort on a ship, even in the most tumultuous waters, I began to feel my hungry, empty stomach protest this constant treatment with pain and nausea. I rolled on my side and closed my eyes, knowing the only thing I could do was wait out this terrible storm and hope for brighter days ahead.

I must have lain in bed for a terribly long time. When I awoke, the skylight showed me brilliantly blue skies and bright sun overhead. I even thought I heard the call of a bird. Feeling my body's pressing need for attention on many levels, I rose and attended to my toilette for the morning. After rearranging my dirty gown and smoothing back loose hair, a realisation struck me.

The *Lucille* was still. No more pitching and rolling. Then my relief was trumped by concern—the *Lucille* was suspiciously still. Even at anchor in the calmest bay, a boat would still have the feel of water under it. I hurried to the door.

The blinding sun caused me to shade my eyes. After a day of clouds and lightning, this constant blast of sun was shocking. I went to the railing. We were in a natural cove of sorts. The shore was littered with debris from trees. Some trees were even uprooted recently and lying on their sides. Our ship was close to shore, far too close. We were grounded. Grounded hard and deep, if I had to guess. The waves lapping the sides of the boat had no effect to shift her at all. I looked up at the mast, the very first concern when a ship is grounded so severely as I suspected the *Lucille* was. When a ship hits with such force as we must have, very frequently the mast is snapped in two. Miraculously, our ship's mast was intact and standing tall.

I stepped out to the railing and surveyed the rest of the landscape around me. There were no structures to be seen anywhere. The port city of Bridgetown was nowhere to be seen. Was this still even Barbados?

I glanced around, hoping to catch sight of Captain Price. The crew were shifting and lugging broken spars and torn sails that had been ripped away from their lashings by the force of the wind. I realised that we were very lucky to even be alive.

My stomach, neglected so completely for so very long, protested loudly and a feeling of faintness swept over me. I turned to the hatch to descend below for food and to check on the welfare of Midshipman Ross. I hoped that he had broken through his fever enough to have weathered the storm well.

"Midshipman Ross! You are sitting up! I am very pleased to see you doing better and having made it through the storm so tolerably."

The poor man was gaunt and had lost some of his hair from his bout with yellow fever. But weight could be regained and hats and wigs employed. The fact that he was alive and sitting up was very promising. He furrowed his brows at my entrance, discomfited by the attention of the wife of a high-ranking officer.

"Mrs Wentworth!"

He made a move to stand and I held up my hand.

"Please, Mr Ross, you would cause me no end of anxiety if you attempted to rise. Please, tell me, how do you feel?"

"Better, ma'am. I think the storm caused me to wake and rally more than it did harm to me."

"That is excellent! Then the *Lucille* weathered the storm for a very good cause, if your recovery is the result."

He smiled sheepishly. Then another look of concern returned to his eyes. "But you, Mrs Wentworth, would not be here if it were not for me and the need to quarantine the ship. I am so sorry."

I laid my palm on top of his skeletal, limp hand. Gently, I whispered, "Belay that talk, sailor. I am the wife of a captain, and I know very well the risks involved in stepping aboard a ship."

A smile of relief spread over his wan face. I smiled back at him and promised to fetch him a cup of tea. When I returned, I encouraged him to dip his bread in the tea to soften it and eat as much as he could bear to.

Mr Cole entered. "Ah, Mrs Wentworth, I see the storm had little effect on you. Half the crew has been sick to their stomachs with the tossing around of the ship."

"I am sorry to hear that."

"Yes, well. Cannot be helped, I suppose. Ross, I see your favourite visitor has come to call. Mrs Wentworth was very attentive to you during the worst of your illness. Brought you some special tea, read to you, held your hand while you ranted."

Mr Ross, horrified at the impropriety of this image, started a stuttered apology.

I quickly assured him that I had helped ship doctors on numerous occasions. "You have no need for embarrassment. I feel it my duty to help those in pain."

"She was even here when you called out the name of a

certain person named Susan? Does that sound familiar, Ross?" the doctor teased.

We both had the gratification to see a faint blush of colour return to his cheek. If he was strong enough to experience a hint of embarrassment, there was little doubt that he would make a full recovery. Feeling that Ross's discomfort at my presence was not helping him, I excused myself and went to the galley for a bite to eat.

Later, up on deck, I watched the longboats as the men laboured to pull *Lucille* out of her grounding. The sails were set and the men strained hard at the oars, but she stubbornly refused to budge. Eventually, the lowering of the tide made it a futile exercise and the boats returned to *Lucille*. I saw a very tired-looking Captain Price, his young face worn and sagging, and approached him.

"Have you had an opportunity for some sleep, Captain?"

"Ah, yes. That is, I did sleep for a few hours this morning when the tide was low and the men were repairing the rigging."

"It seems that all is looking better than it was at first light," I said as I glanced up at the rigging. A few sails were unfurled, but not all. Too strong a wind on masts that could not move would snap the masts in two. Price was doing his best to keep additional damage to a minimum. "I am glad the grounding of the ship was not so severe as to cause the mast to break off."

"Yes, it is a reason for gratitude. The force with which we struck this sandbar could have easily dismasted us. Perhaps you would be more comfortable if we set up a tent for you on the beach?"

"If I am no trouble, I would rather stay on board, with your permission of course."

He grinned at me and some of the care of the last several days fled his countenance. "I am happy to have you stay with the crew, Mrs Wentworth. You helped Midshipman Ross pull through as quickly as he did. And young Stanley, the ship's boy who plays the fife, is quite taken with you, I believe."

"Stanley is as bright as a new farthing."

"We should have a schoolmaster for him and the younger crewmembers, but none could be found when we were last in England."

"I should imagine it will not be long before my own son will be wanting to enlist." I sighed.

"Once the sea is in your blood, ma'am, it is difficult to think of anything else."

I returned to my cabin to look around at the havoc wrought by the storm. I stripped the bedding off and laid it out on deck to dry alongside the many hammocks that the sailors were attempting to dry out as well. After a bit of restoration, I opened my trunk and placed the letters from Frederick within, saving the very last out for me to read. They had been safely tucked away in my dress during the most chaotic moments of the storm. If I was to go to the bottom of the sea, I would have had this precious correspondence with me.

I leant over to right the deadly chair from the ground and discovered, in a pool of seawater, the melted, running letters from Mary and Lady Russell. I bit my lip at that oversight. I picked up the papers with their running ink and laid them flat upon the table. There was some hope that they would survive, but it was unlikely.

I sat on the chair and unfolded the last letter from Frederick.

Dear Anne,

As strange a development as this was never to be seen. I have not been terribly faithful to you in my letters over the last several years due to the simple reason that I am trying to forget you. That is impossible. But I may, by lessening the time I spend writing letters to you that I shall never send, make you a smaller presence in my thoughts. The results of this policy for myself have been mixed in terms of success.

Now, in some sort of unimaginable cruelty, Kellynch Hall is to be let by your father, and none other than my own dear sister Sophia and Admiral Croft are to take it. In fact, they already have taken it and may very well be moving in as I write. I have just received a very warm letter from Sophy inviting me to stay with them as their guest at Kellynch Hall in Somersetshire for as long as I want or am able. Napoleon has been banished to Elba and the war is over. In the very near future, as soon as we make port and our leave is approved, I shall be a man of leisure.

The Crofts viewed Kellynch as a very fine manor house in a county that they have heard is very lovely by myself and our brother. They are little aware that it holds both dear and painful memories for me. To walk into the very parlour where your father looked at me with such undisguised disdain as I applied for your hand, I hardly know how I shall feel.

Am I a fool to accept their invitation? I believe not, as the Crofts seem to think that your family is to remove to Bath. That must indeed be a trial for you, Anne. I know how bitter the city of Bath makes you feel, as you have unhappy memories associated with it from the loss of your dear mother. I am exceedingly grateful that you will not be staying in the neighbour-hood with Lady Russell. To be forced into company with the both of you would be too much for me to bear.

I cannot write how I shall react to seeing all the places where we had so many instances of true happiness together, Anne. I am reeling from the improbability of it all. But perhaps all this speculation of mine is for naught. You may be happily married and living elsewhere altogether. I will not expose myself to the well-intentioned questions of my older sister by demanding information on each of the Elliot ladies.

It will be a test of how well I have inured myself to the idea of life without you, Anne. That thought still runs a shudder down my spine, but I have accustomed myself to it. Even if you are unmarried still, the idea that you could have held fast to our love for eight long years is highly unlikely. Even a very stupid fellow must see how extraordinary a woman you are. I am quite sure you have had other offers.

If we meet and I find you unmarried still, I will hold tight to my heart and not allow myself to fall into any conversation of depth with you. I cannot survive another wrenching of my heart by you. We shall speak only of the most mundane topics. Topics we used to avoid at dinner parties and dances. The weather. The fitness of the roads for travel. The health of the local parson. Should we meet again, I shall never venture into any conversation of meaning or humour with you. To do so would mean risking a long, deep look into those eyes.

I will instead turn my sight to all the unmarried young ladies that the county of Somersetshire must surely be populated with. I am not the unworthy prospect for unattached women that I was years ago. At the very least, it will be great fun to dance and laugh and sing again. I am not such an old man as to turn my nose up at the thought of those entertainments. No, indeed, I am not.

I can safely write that I am very near to being completely recovered from my attachment to you. All that I need to complete the process and close that dark chapter of my life completely is the company of a lively young lady to marvel at my tales of adventures on the high seas. It is regrettable that it will most likely be a lady without the sharp mind you possess to challenge me when my boast seems too unlikely or to quote a certain historian or piece of poetry to broaden my understanding of the world. It pains me to end this letter so, but I can no longer preface my name with 'Yours' or any other romantic endearments. I must sign plain and simply.

Respectfully,
Captain Frederick Wentworth
HMS Laconia

Despite the thousands of warm, loving words that Frederick had spoken to me since writing that letter so many years ago, it still pained my chest to read what was before me—to imagine him building such a careful, cold wall around his heart to protect himself from an unlikely encounter with me. How rapidly the first cracks must have begun to shatter his resolve upon our meeting again at Uppercross and his first words about me to my sister Mary.

"Captain Wentworth is not very gallant by you, Anne, though he was so attentive to me... He said, 'You were so altered he should not have known you again.'"

How much of that statement had been in an effort to preserve the strength of his resolve? I had no doubt that many years of reflection and regret had indeed altered me from the blooming youth of nineteen who had first caught his eye. The intervening years of adventure and hardship had served to make Frederick even more distinguished and dashing than he had been as a youthful, newly made master and commander. Upon reflection, I could honestly say that my heart had been completely unchanged when I first saw him again at Uppercross. No matter how I had tutored myself privately in my thoughts on the probability of an impending union between Frederick and Louisa, I had still felt a thrill of excitement every time he entered a room. The falsehoods we had both told ourselves, it was all a ridiculous parody of the truth that was before both of our eyes. We had lost even more time to misunderstanding and pride. Foolish.

Tears fell on the precious letter and I wiped them away with the sleeve of my grimy gown lest the ink should be made to run. With a wry smile, I looked over at the swirled and blasted black ink smeared over the neglected letters from Mary and Lady Russell. Ah well, it was unintentionally done. Or was it?

CHAPTER TWENTY-NINE

The next morning was again a lovely day. Blue skies and perfectly white billowing clouds were racing by the skylight of the cabin. There was no trace of the brutal weather that had landed us on the beach. A deep rumbling of rolling barrels and winches met my ear. It sounded as if the ship was being unloaded of its cargo. I left the shadow of my cabin and entered the brilliant sunshine of the morning.

Once again, the men had the longboats out and were straining to free the *Lucille* with the high tide. Sails billowed and the groan of the mast could be heard underneath the whistling hum of the wind through the rigging. Captain Price looked towards the boats, then up to the mast, worry on his brow as he tried to judge what was the correct amount of sail to unfurl while not risking the snapping of the mast.

"Good morning, Captain Price. How do your efforts to loosen the ship progress?"

"Not well. I have the men carrying the stores ashore to

lessen the weight of the ship. If that is unsuccessful, we shall take the cannons ashore as well."

"Is not that risky? In case we are not on Barbados or discovered by unfriendly forces?"

"I have little choice. As we are grounded, you see, with the aft sticking out, we would be unable to defend ourselves."

"Will you be taking the furniture from your cabin ashore?"

"If it comes to that, yes. We shall try to float her off again tomorrow morning with as little weight as possible. Even the crew will be ashore."

Later in the day, when I came back on deck, the men had moved most of the cargo to the beach and were in the process of shifting the deck cannons there as well to be set up as a precautionary source of cannon fire. The crew was working hard in the full power of the sun's heat to ensure the ship would be as light as possible for the next high tide attempt to refloat the *Lucille*. A small band of men—one officer and a couple of marines and seamen—were on the beach, organising packs that lay open on the ground. No doubt the captain had waited to launch an expedition inland until most of the cargo had been shifted.

"Should we move the square piano as well, Captain Price?" I enquired. "It could be easily transferred to the beach, if you think it best."

"What? Oh, pardon, Mrs Wentworth," he said as he turned to me with his tired eyes. "I doubt that the piano is adding significantly to our heft. If we are on a populated island—Barbados, if we are fortunate, but I doubt it—the men will ferret out some aid for us. I know how precious a piano is in this part of the world, so no need to risk it. I greatly appreciate your offer, though."

"You do not believe us to be on Barbados?"

"By my calculations from the night stars, I believe us to be somewhere west of Barbados. Perhaps St Vincent or the Grenadines. If it is some out of the way spot, not populated, we may be in for a long stay. The boatswain has suggested a system of rope and tackle attached to trees that may aid in pulling us loose. Let us hope this reduction in weight will cause the ship to shift free next high tide."

I nodded and moved away, knowing how strained he was with the many attempts to float the *Lucille*. I leant against the balustrade and gazed towards the sea. I had never before experienced so uncertain a time as this when aboard a ship. My heart strained towards the open sea and the intense longing to be reunited with my children and husband. For the first time, I indulged in allowing a tear to course down my cheek as my heart called out for Frederick.

Through my blurred vision, as if in response to my silent plea, I saw the top of a mast emerge from the treetops on the shore closest to the open sea. I gasped and pointed.

"Captain Price!"

A commotion erupted behind me of swift footsteps and orders. Price shouted up to the man in the crow's nest, demanding an identification of the ship we could not fully view yet.

"Pirates!"

An explosion of orders followed. I slid out of the way as the crew manned the two small cannons at the aft of the ship. Captain Price shouted to the cannons on land that had just been moved into place. Then he placed his hand firmly on mine and manoeuvred me away from the ship's aft.

"Mrs Wentworth, I had rather that ship not see a lady on

deck, if you don't mind. You should go ashore to the expedition party."

I nodded and ran to the cabin to retrieve my letters from Frederick. They were placed in the bodice of my dress while I also grabbed some biscuits and a flask of wine wrapped in a shawl. I exited the cabin and recoiled to see the massive pirate ship of at least seventy-four guns round the corner to enter our small bay. My heart cried out for the men who would stay and fight to the last against these marauders. In a flash of inspiration, I looked up to see what colours we flew. A ragged Union Jack flew there, barely more than a few strands. The yellow jack flags were gone, dissolved and ripped away by the force of the storm. Remembering something in one of Frederick's letters, I turned back to the cabin.

I rifled through my trunk like a mad woman, flinging everything aside in an effort to gain my prize. I pulled up my yellow gown. It was very similar to the one I had worn the first time I danced with Frederick and his heart made his feet as heavy as workhorse hooves. I had taken it everywhere with me since reading that letter of Frederick's, knowing it to be his favourite colour on me. I grabbed a knife from the desk and began to tear it to shreds. At last, I raised as large a square from it as I could muster.

Stanley popped into the doorway. "Captain says I'm to escort you on shore, ma'am. Afore the pirates get here, make quick!"

I knew we had a few minutes, as the wind was weak and the pirate ship's progress would be slow. I exited the cabin, crouching down in an attempt to stay out of view of the oncoming ship.

"Take this to Captain Price. Tell him to run it up under the Union Jack." I handed Stanley the yellow fabric. He stared at it for a moment, puzzled, before understanding lit his eyes.

"Yes, ma'am!"

I glanced at the approaching ship that was entering the bay. They were lowering their boats into the water. Stanley spoke to the captain and shoved the shred of my yellow gown towards him. He nodded Stanley towards the Union Jack. The boy ran to the base of the ropes, hauled down the Union Jack, attached the gown piece I had given him, and raised it back up.

Would the pirate ship believe it was not a deception? I wrung my hands, not knowing if they would suspect deceit and risk the lives of their men to take our ship and its cargo. Perhaps we could add another layer to the scene of our ship. I called to Stanley to come to me again.

"Stanley, help me to go below decks, I shall crouch along beside you."

"But you are to go ashore! Captain's orders!"

"Lend me your hand, please."

He sighed loudly and walked in front of me as we scurried to the stairs. We went to the medical bay and awoke a sleeping Midshipman Ross. I told him he was needed on deck and why. He shakily came up to his feet, and with the support of myself and Stanley, we made our way to the stairs.

Step by step, we slowly climbed up. Stanley above lent Ross the help of a hand and me behind, steadying him. He made his way, as wobbly as a new colt, to the deck. The shine of the sun made him recoil briefly before pressing ahead.

"Now, help him to the rail, Stanley. Make sure he is fully visible to the pirate ship."

If there had been doubt in the mind of the marauders as to the truth of our improvised yellow flag, the sight of a clearly weak, pale Midshipman Ross through a spyglass would make them reconsider. Peeking over the edge of the hatch, I saw that the boats from the pirate ship did not proceed closer. The ship dropped anchor, their plan undoubtedly being to wait us out. They would not risk cannon fire destroying such a choice prize as a British naval ship.

While the afternoon weighed on heavily and the shadows grew long, I knew that sometime in the night, I should have to make my way onto shore and escape with the party assembled there. The thought of abandoning the ship and men to the bloodthirsty cutthroats did not sit well with me, but the alternatives were too terrible to contemplate.

As I sat on the edge of the bunk, a wave of despair at the now very real thought of never seeing my children or husband again pressed upon me. My hand reached for the warm bulge of papers that were still nestled in the bosom of my gown. I tried to remember the instances of Frederick's courage in the face of danger. It calmed me. I inhaled deeply and decided to make for the shore as soon as dusk fell so that the party could slip away when they saw fit.

In the deepening of the shadows of the waning day, a cry broke free from the man in the crow's nest.

"Ship!"

I ran to the door and looked out. Along the same path the previous mast had taken, another mast skimmed the tree-tops. All aboard the *Lucille* waited, frozen in place as more of the masts came into sight. There was a fleck of blue, then a fleck of red. Then a huge Union Jack emerged over the lowering horizon of trees. A cry erupted from everyone aboard as the beautiful sight of the HMS *Stoic* rounded the corner. As soon as she was able, the fore cannons blasted a round for the pirate ship. Little damage was caused by those few cannons, but it threw the enemy ship into disarray. The pirate ship opened fire on us and the *Stoic* simultaneously, but to little effect.

Captain Price gave the command for the cannons he had

placed on the aft of the ship, as well as those on shore, to open fire. It was a small volley, but one that added to the anxiety of the pirate ship. Until the *Stoic* could draw up alongside and release a full broadside, the combined efforts of the two British ships were enough to throw them off their stride.

The *Stoic* sailed between the pirate ship and ours and let loose all the cannons on her starboard side. An explosion of dense smoke and the shattering of wood echoed around the small harbour.

"Lower the boats!" Price cried. "All men. Prepare to board the enemy ship!"

Every crewman, excepting the doctor, Midshipman Ross, and myself, emptied into the boats and began to row across to the pirate ship. After another broadside from the *Stoic* directly into the pirate ship, I could hear the shouts and flurry of boarding parties climbing aboard. Soon, from across the bay, the sound of pistol fire and clashing swords reached my ears as Ross and I stood on the aft of the ship, trying to catch a glimpse of the action through the swirl of smoke.

It was a torturous time that felt ceaseless. The heat from the sun, the sound of men screaming—some in triumph, some in pain—the acrid scent of the wafting cloud of cannon smoke. At last, the sounds subsided altogether. The Jolly Roger of the pirate ship was struck, and the Union Jack was run up in its place. Ross and I both cried out in happiness at the change in colours on the pirate ship. Before very long, a boat was being rowed to the *Lucille*. At the bow, a very tall man in a blue coat was leaning into the wind.

"Frederick," I whispered as a sob of relief escaped my mouth.

As soon as he was alongside, he cried up, "Permission to come aboard!"

I paused for a moment, as Ross and I exchanged glances. We both looked to the doctor.

"I believe we are well past the stage of being a danger to others, it has been nearly a week," he said as he nodded.

Ross leant over the railing. "Permission granted, Captain Wentworth."

No sooner had the words left Ross's lips than Frederick was bounding up the rope ladder on the side of the ship. He leapt over the rail and swept me up in a fiercely firm embrace. My feet left the deck as he twirled me in a circle.

"Anne! You are well?"

"Yes, Frederick. Very well indeed, just homesick for my husband and children."

I pulled away from his embrace and saw a still oozing, ugly gash on his cheek. The depth of the wound would leave a noticeable scar on his face long after it healed.

"Frederick! What has happened?"

His brow knit tightly when his hand touched the tender flesh around the wound. He grinned lopsidedly. "I renewed my former acquaintance with Captain Twist. He came out much worse for the meeting. But he left me this souvenir so that every time I see my reflection, until my dying day, I shall remember how close he came to..."

I touched his unwounded cheek and looked into his eyes. "But he did not. I am alive and well, my love." My hand moved lower and stroked his strong chin. "Besides, I have always thought a beard on a man was very becoming."

"Why, Mrs Wentworth, you are full of surprises."

And there, under the flapping remnants of my yellow gown, both of us tired and under the astonished gaze of the crew of the *Lucille* that was climbing back on board, we kissed.

Once we separated, Frederick said, "Do you absolutely

promise me that this will put an end to any solo voyages for you?"

"Absolutely not! I acquitted myself very well indeed. Did you not observe"—I gazed up—"the reason the pirate ship delayed its attack?"

Frederick squinted. "Is that your yellow gown?" He smiled back down at me. "Very resourceful."

"I may make admiral before you, yet," I replied, laughing. "It was your letters, Frederick, which gave me the inspiration. You writing to me all those years ago, it saved us."

"No, Anne. You are mistaken," he replied, his face very serious. "Writing those letters to you saved *me*. More than you can ever know."

It was our silent, mutual consent that since we had already accustomed the busy crew around us to our improper display, they could suffer through one more.

But that was the end of it. Frederick straightened his spine, that shade of inscrutability drew down over his eyes. He stepped away from me and cleared his throat.

"I must find Captain Price and thank him for his service to you."

"Of course." I reached out and grabbed Stanley as he was dashing by. "May I introduce a very worthy seaman, without whose help our deception with the yellow flag may never have succeeded? Captain Wentworth, this is Mr Stanley."

An awestruck Stanley rubbed his hand on the side of his pants and extended it out. Frederick took it and shook it while solemnly commending him for his service. "And I shall make a note of your bravery in my ship's log, young man. I will also make certain to note the progress of your career in the coming years."

A greater look of sincere joy could not have been found on another ship in the navy.

"Now, Anne, let's retrieve the blasted, um, the lovely

square piano that was the cause of all of this and row you back to the *Stoic*. It may take us some time to float the *Lucille* free, and I am sure that you would be more at ease on the *Stoic*."

"You mean out of Captain Price's way, do you not? I am quite sure that he will be very glad to return to his cabin."

And so, after loading my small trunk—excepting one yellow gown and my copy of *Rob Roy* which I left for Stanley —and the square piano aboard a longboat, we sailed past the dark ship of the late Captain Twist and towards the *Stoic*. Never was I happier to feel the boards of a ship under my feet and to stand at the side of my husband as we faced future adventures of letters, sailing, and music together. And I swore to always have in my possession a gown of yellow. It seemed to bring me tremendously good fortune.

The End

ACKNOWLEDGMENTS

Thank you so much to Quills & Quartos Publishing for taking a chance on a quirky, swashbuckling *Persuasion* sequel from an unpublished writer. I feel like understanding some of Naval life during the Regency era is a big part of appreciating why the character of Captain Frederick Wentworth was so beloved by both Anne Elliot and Jane Austen. The encouragement I received from Quills & Quartos pushed me to enrich and expand what I started as just a quick short story.

A big thanks to my two beta readers, James Ferrell and Sally Zeigler, who eagerly awaited new installments being delivered by snail mail.

Thank you, Brad Constable, for helping me find the time and space needed to finish this book.

Thank you to C. S. Forester, author of the *Horatio Hornblower* series, which I adore. If you want an excellent historical fiction series of Naval life in the Regency era, I highly recommend starting with *Mr Midshipman Hornblower*.

Thanks to Allison Crews, Jennifer Bolt and Sara Mullins-Spears for the good vibes, Indian food, peppermint cups, and JAFF FB page suggestions.

And, of course, thank you, Jane.

ABOUT THE AUTHOR

Lyndsay Constable is a Taurus Sun/Scorpio Rising who runs a small vegetable farm in Virginia with her husband. She has loved Jane Austen since her teens and often ponders 'what would Jane do?' If she is ever stuck for an idea, you can find her in the fields picking kale or digging up sweet potatoes or watering the greenhouse–or a myriad of other activities that keep the farm running and help her organize her muddled thoughts. She is an excellent walker.

Manufactured by Amazon.ca
Acheson, AB